THE SCALP OF IRON EYES

Infamous bounty hunter Iron Eyes steers his palomino stallion through hostile terrain, eager to get his hands on the outlaws who have their images on the crumpled wanted posters in his deep pockets. His bullet-coloured eyes catch a glimpse of Ten Strike, and he knows his pursuit is coming to an end. The trouble is that there are men within the remote settlement who have waited for the gaunt horseman with their guns cocked and ready. Soon Iron Eyes will be fighting for his life . . .

RORY BLACK

---◆---

THE SCALP OF IRON EYES

Complete and Unabridged

LINFORD
Leicester

First published in Great Britain in 2016 by
Robert Hale
an imprint of The Crowood Press
Wiltshire

First Linford Edition
published 2019
by arrangement with
The Crowood Press
Wiltshire

A catalogue record for this book is available
from the British Library.

ISBN 978–1–4448–4106–0

Published by
F. A. Thorpe (Publishing)
Anstey, Leicestershire

Set by Words & Graphics Ltd.
Anstey, Leicestershire
Printed and bound in Great Britain by
T. J. International Ltd., Padstow, Cornwall

This book is printed on acid-free paper

Dedicated with love to Gary
and Karen George

Prologue

Squirrel Sally Cooke was a girl on a mission and that mission was to sink her talons on the man she sought. For the umpteenth time, Iron Eyes had disappeared after renting a hotel room for them both and then abandoned her there as he chased after fresh wanted outlaws. Once again, the bounty hunter had set out to claim the blood money on their heads and forgotten to mention it to his female companion.

Yet Sally was like a seasoned blood hound. She was not easily put off the scent. She had tracked the emaciated man for more than sixty miles across country atop the ramshackle stagecoach she had purchased a year earlier.

The six-horse team pulled the embattled stage-coach along the mountain-tain trail as the feisty female cracked her bullwhip above their heads. The powerful black horses had worked hard to pull the hefty vehicle up the steep, twisting trail road for nearly thirty minutes before the expert hands of Squirrel Sally steered them over the precarious ridge and down the other side of the mountain.

The rough trail, which at times fringed the very edge of the steep mountains, had been forged through the ocean of trees by necessity rather than grand design by the lumberjacks who needed a road they could transport their wagons along to the outside world.

One false move could spell disaster and send them toppling into the green abyss but Sally was unafraid as she guided both team and coach to the very brink of the mountain trail. The vehicle's metal wheel rims skimmed the loose gravel as they taunted potential death.

The crude road had never been meant for anything apart from the long logging wagons to use, yet the young female who sat high on the stagecoach's driver's seat was unafraid and continued to drive her sturdy team of horses along its treacherous trail at a perilous pace.

Her beautiful eyes squinted down into the valley to where she could just make out the logging town through the shimmering heat haze. As she slapped the hefty reins across the backs of her charging team, she wondered if her beloved Iron Eyes might be there, hunting out his chosen prey. The stagecoach skidded on its wheel rims around another acute bend in the trail as it quickly descended the slope.

Clouds of dust flew up into the blue sky from the hoofs of the muscular horses as she wrestled with the long leathers and brake pole beneath her bare foot.

Sally would not allow the exhausted horses to rest until she had navigated her way down the mountainside. She gave out a bellowing cry of encouragement as the coach rocked on its axles.

Few grown men had the ability to control a stagecoach with such ease and even fewer had the courage to attempt to cross the dangerous trail that had been carved out of the mountainside.

The diminutive young Sally had only one thing on her mind and that was to find her man. Everything else was unimportant to her as she continued to drive her lathered-up team through the blazing sunlight toward the sprawling settlement in the valley. Unlike the majority of females in the West, Sally was totally oblivious to how a young lady was expected to behave or act.

Her feistiness was only equalled by her innocence.

As her gloved hands cracked the bullwhip over the heads of her six horses, she was totally unaware that the arduous task of controlling her team had virtually turned her trail gear into torn rags. Every button on her sweat-soaked shirt had parted company with its worn fabric, revealing far more than

4

she realized as she energetically drove the stagecoach down toward the town.

Curiously, Sally looked at the town she was heading into and eased back on her reins and started to push down on the brake pole. The horses started to slow as the stagecoach reached level ground. She shook her dusty head of long golden curls and studied the town carefully.

One thing was obvious. This town was unlike any other she had ever entered. Sally was confused at the sight of mountains of trimmed lumber stacked on both sides of the solitary street she was guiding her exhausted horses along.

Large muscular lumberjacks emerged from every corner of the town at the unexpected sound of the stagecoach. They stared in disbelief at the sight of a new female entering their remote settlement. Every eye watched Sally as she expertly steered the long vehicle down the dusty street.

None of them had imagined that they

would wake up to the beautiful sight of a near naked female driving a battle-scarred stagecoach. She unintentionally lured them toward her without even realizing it.

Sally slowed the stagecoach as it travelled along the main street. Within minutes of her arrival, a hundred well-built men watched as she guided the team toward a large livery stable. A half-dozen large logging wagons surrounded the stable.

It was obvious to Sally that this was a lumber town. A place which relied for its very survival upon the trees its menfolk could cut, trim and send out of the valley. The bare patches of forest along the route she had travelled to reach this settlement had told her that much.

As the battered stage ground to a halt outside the stable, Sally observed the muscular men watching her every feminine movement with grateful eyes.

She secured the brake pole and looped the long leathers around its length as her eyes darted around the gathering.

A lot of womenfolk might have been nervous when faced with so many lustful men but not Squirrel Sally. Nothing had ever succeeded in frightening the confident young female.

Sally remained on the driver's seat and removed her gloves as she pulled her primed pipe from her torn pants pocket and gripped its stem between her teeth.

As she watched them through her mane of golden curls, the men started to move toward her. It was like being surrounded by ravenous timber wolves. Sally scratched a match across the brake pole and lit her pipe. As smoke billowed from its bowl and her mouth, she reached down and pulled her trusty Winchester up from inside the driver's box.

Sally cranked its mechanism. A metal casing flew over her bare shoulder from its magazine as she lowered its gleaming barrel and aimed down at the men who had been encroaching on her high vantage place.

The sound of the rifle being readied stopped every one of the men in their tracks. Their startled expressions amused the petite female as she puffed feverishly on her pipe.

Faster than spit, she fired and cocked her trusty carbine three times. The bullets kicked up dust a few feet before their boot leather and showered sand over them.

'That's as close as any of you hairy critters are gonna get. Savvy?' she yelled. 'Any of you frisky bastards try to get any closer and I'll split your skulls with hot lead.'

She stood and rested one foot on the rim of the box as she faced the curious men. None of the large lumberjacks had ever seen anything quite so small or dangerous before.

Sally tossed her hair off her face and then plucked her pipe from her lips. Her eyes levelled at them.

'Don't think I don't know what you

horn-toads got on your minds,' she shouted at them as they encircled the stagecoach curiously. 'I seen that frisky look before but I'm betrothed and don't hanker for nothing but information. All I wanna know is where my beloved is. Any of you lust-buckets seen a useless critter on a mighty fine palomino stallion?'

None of the men replied.

They just studied the defiant female with the smoking Winchester rifle in her hands and lusted at the desirable sight before them.

Sally dropped her pipe on the driver's seat and cranked the mechanism again.

'I asked you a question,' she riled.

One of the lumberjacks took a step closer to the stagecoach and tilted his head back like a rooster vainly trying to impress a hen.

'How old are you, sweet cheeks?' he shouted across the distance between them. 'You sure look old enough to make a man obliged.'

Sally squinted as she raised the rifle

to her shoulder and aimed at him.

'I'm old enough, you ugly bastard,' she hissed through gritted teeth. 'Old enough to part you from your hair.'

Laughter erupted among the crowd.

Another of the excited lumberjacks scratched his head.

'What's the name of this man you're looking for, missy?' he called out. 'If'n he's real, that is.'

Without any warning Sally fired. The town shook to the sound of the rifle as a fiery rod of lethal venom spewed from its barrel and cut through the dry air. The lumberjack yelped like a whipped dog.

He grabbed his bleeding ear as he realized that a chunk of it had just been separated from his head. The crowd roared even louder at the sight of the determined young female with the smoking rifle in her hands.

'Nobody calls Squirrel Sally a liar,' she spat.

The wounded lumberjack stared in disbelief at her. 'You done shot half my ear off, you little vixen.'

Sally then cocked the Winchester again and lowered her aim until she had the weapon trained on the bulge in his filthy pants.

'You just keep talking and bleeding and I'll put my next bullet in your brains,' she warned and then grinned. 'I'm told most men think with what the sweet Lord put in their long-johns.'

The bleeding lumberjack turned on his heels and marched away from the stagecoach. He disappeared from view, leaving only a crimson trail of bloody droplets in his wake.

'Has any of you hairy hombres seen my man?' Sally repeated angrily before adding, 'I'm getting a tad impatient with you boys not answering me.'

One of the larger of the men held his hands up as if in surrender and bravely moved toward Squirrel Sally. He stopped advancing just below the driver's box and looked up at the tiny firecracker.

'What's the name of your man, little

lady?' he asked in a low, quiet tone. 'Maybe he has bin here.'

Sally sat back down on the long seat and picked up a whiskey bottle as she rested the rifle on her hip. She pulled the cork with her teeth and took a mouthful of the strong liquor. Lowering the bottle, she stared down at the one lumberjack that did not seem to underestimate her.

'Iron Eyes,' she told him. 'His name's Iron Eyes the bounty hunter. Has any of you hairy bastards heard of him?'

The smiles faded from the faces of the burly men. Each one of them knew of the bounty hunter by reputation and felt fortunate that they had never encountered him. Sally watched them slowly disperse until only the brave lumberjack remained standing beside the stable wall.

'Have you seen him?' Sally asked.

The lumberjack shook his head and sighed heavily. 'I'm right sorry, darling. As far as I know he ain't bin here.'

Sally stared at the bearded face. 'You

have heard of him though, ain't you?'

He nodded.

'Sure I have. I reckon there ain't many folks that ain't heard of him, little lady,' he said. 'They call him the living ghost, I hear.'

'He ain't here?' Sally sounded disappointed.

'We ain't had no burials lately so I reckon he ain't bin here,' the man replied as he slowly lowered his hands. 'You seem to be looking real hard for your man.'

For a few moments she just sat cradling the bottle and her rifle. Then she sighed heavily and looked at the bearded man standing below her.

She nodded.

'Yep, I am looking real hard,' she muttered.

The large man toyed with his beard.

'The sheriff might have himself a notion of where he is, ma'am,' the lumberjack said, pointing down the street. 'He keeps a close eye on folks in these parts. He might know where your

Iron Eyes is. We got ourselves a brand new telegraph office.'

Sally replaced the cork into the bottle neck and then climbed down to the boardwalk and looked into the livery stable. Her keen eyes spotted the blacksmith hiding within its confines.

'Hey you. Tend to my team,' she demanded before tossing a few coins into the blacksmith's hands. 'And leave my bottle of rye alone.'

The lumberjack nervously backed away from Sally as she rested the rifle on her shoulder but kept her finger curled around its trigger.

'How come the sheriff didn't come looking to see who was doing all the shooting?' Sally wondered.

'I said he was a good sheriff,' the lumberjack shrugged. 'I didn't say he was suicidal.'

Sally laughed and walked close to the massive lumberjack as they started along the street. She leaned back and looked up into his bearded face.

'You gotta name?' she asked.

'Buck,' he nervously answered.

She nodded. 'They call me Squirrel Sally.'

'And Iron Eyes is your man?' he wondered.

'He sure is.' Sally smiled as she rested the barrel of the Winchester on her slim shoulder. 'The trouble is he keeps on running away, Buck. Why do you reckon a varmint would do that?'

'Maybe he's scared of you.' Buck grinned.

A wicked smile crossed her beautiful dust-caked face. She liked the suggestion. They continued toward the sheriff's small wooden office standing beside the telegraph office.

'Reckon I might have to scare your sheriff,' she said. 'All I want you to do is to stand behind me real quiet like.'

He nodded. 'It'll be a pleasure, little lady.'

They walked down the boardwalk side by side in the direction of the sheriff's office. Buck Smith towered over the tiny female like one of the giant trees he chopped down for a living. And just like the trees, Buck was fully aware that the fearless Squirrel Sally could cut him down to size any time she chose.

Sheriff Bob Kane looked up from his desk blotter at the tiny female who barged into his office with the lumber-jack on her heels.

The lawman was startled.

'What in tarnation is going on here?' Kane stared at Sally in bewilderment. He blinked hard as if attempting to clear his eyes of the sight of the beautiful female covered in trail dust and very little else apart from ill-fitting torn pants and a shirt open to her belly button.

Normally he would have arrested any female so scantily clad in his town but the rifle on her shoulder changed his mind. Smoke still curled out of its long barrel.

Kane stared at her as she marched up to his desk and swung the Winchester down until it was aimed at his face. He leaned back in his chair and sniffed the scent of gunpowder trailing from its barrel.

'Buck here tells me that you might know where my betrothed is, Sheriff,' she snarled. 'Do you? Do you know where my Iron Eyes is?'

'Iron Eyes?' Kane repeated the infamous name. 'Are you looking for Iron Eyes?'

Sally pushed the barrel into the lawman's throat. 'Do you know where he is? I'm looking for him. You'd best tell me or this town is gonna have to hire themselves a new star packer.'

'Calm down, little lady,' Kane croaked.

'I'll calm down after you answer my question,' Sally snorted.

Kane slowly raised his hand and brushed the metal barrel of the Winchester aside and then mopped his brow with the tails of his bandanna.

'I'll tell you, young 'un,' he stammered. 'I was wired a few hours back. Iron Eyes is hot on the trail of the

17

Brooks gang and headed to Ten Strike.'

Sally leapt up onto the desk and kept the rifle trained on the lawman. Her eyes were burning into the nervous sheriff.

'Who wired you, Sheriff?' she snarled.

'Iron Eyes sent the wire himself.' Kane picked up the scrap of paper and nervously handed it to the rifle-toting female. 'Read it for yourself.'

Sally's eyes narrowed angrily. 'What's it say?'

Realizing that she probably could not read too well, Kane glanced at the short message and then stared into her eyes.

'It says he's after the Brooks boys and wants to know if I was authorized to pay the bounty on their dead carcasses, missy,' Kane mumbled.

Her expression suddenly softened. She lowered the rifle and then jumped back down on to the floorboards. Her head turned, sending her golden locks cascading over her slender shoulders.

'Where's Ten Strike, Buck?' she asked the lumberjack.

'There's a trail cut out through the forest, Sally,' he replied, pointing to the west of town. 'It leads straight there but it's a mighty dangerous trail.'

'Getting here weren't no picnic,' she stated.

'The trail to Ten Strike is even more dangerous, Sally,' Buck warned the female. 'Especially if'n you're driving a stagecoach.'

Sally exhaled angrily and stomped her foot on the boards.

'Damn it all. Anyone would think that varmint is trying to keep away from me,' she snapped. 'Don't he know that I love him?'

They remained silent. Neither the sheriff nor the lumberjack was willing to contradict the upset female when she had her rifle cocked.

Sally ran her fingers over her barely concealed breasts as they searched for and found a few coins in her shirt pocket. She picked them up and shook a fist at the crowd.

'I'm gonna buy a fresh team of horse flesh and head for Ten Strike,' she growled.

Both men watched as Squirrel Sally marched out of the office and headed back toward the livery stable. Bob Kane looked at the towering lumberjack and then nervously moved from his chair to his open door. The sheriff peered around the doorframe as she stalked down the street. His eyes focused on her youthful rear. He then mopped the sweat from his upper lip and shook his head.

'Who the hell was that little twister, Buck?' he asked as he rested his back against the wall. 'She plumb scared the life out of me.'

Buck ran his mighty hand over his beard and sighed.

'She said her name was Squirrel Sally, Bob,' he wistfully replied. 'What a gal.'

'No wonder Iron Eyes keeps his distance from that firecracker, Buck,'

Kane said. 'That little gal is plumb frightening.'

'Sure got herself a mighty fine rump, though, Bob.' Buck sighed heavily.

The lawman raised his eyebrows. 'She also got a darn big split in her pants, Buck. I kinda noticed when she hopped up on my desk.'

The lumberjack chuckled. 'It's a good thing she didn't notice that you noticed, Sheriff.'

Bob Kane walked to his desk, opened its top drawer and pulled out a bottle of whiskey and two glasses. He placed them on his ink blotter and pulled the cork from the bottle neck.

He was about to fill the glasses with the amber nectar when he paused thoughtfully.

'I sure wish I'd been wearing my spectacles, Buck.' He sighed.

1

With the coming of nightfall, the blistering heat of day disappeared across the vast untamed territory and was replaced by a deathly chill. The contrast in temperature had claimed countless lives over the years as unwary travellers fell foul of its merciless severity. Within hours of sundown, frost covered the countless trees and glistened in the moonlight that managed to break through the forest canopy.

An eerie blue haze spread like a cancer across the vast terrain in all directions as a few unholy horsemen guided their mounts through the night fog in search of their next unsuspecting victims.

Ten Strike was well hidden by towering trees which encircled its scattering of brick and wooden structures. It was a place where only those who knew of its existence ever dared to try and locate it. It was also a town which had escaped the sordid reality that plagued the rest of the West.

The three frost-covered figures rode slowly through the surrounding mist into the unlit outskirts of the small settlement. They straightened up and shook the sparkling frost which covered their dishevelled forms from their bodies. They shared a knowing smile as their eyes darted around the innocent town.

Soon that innocence would be destroyed by the trio of horsemen. That was their way. The only way they knew how to survive was to kill before they were killed. It did not matter to them who suffered as long as they themselves came out as victors.

The Brooks gang had once been one of the most lethal and skilful bands of bank robbers in the vast territory. They had struck like phantoms, leaving empty bank vaults and lakes of blood in their wake.

For just over a year, the gang had seemed untouchable and went on from one brutal caper to the next. For a short while they had been regarded as the next James gang.

Then Ben Brooks had made the fateful decision which would cost him and his trusty followers dearly. A hundred miles east of Ten Strike had sealed their downfall when the towns-folk recognized one of the Brooks men as he had ridden in to study the bank carefully before reporting back to his fellow outlaws.

Knowing the reputation of the gang, the town soon armed themselves and waited to trap the villainous bank robbers in a lethal crossfire.

The wanted bank robbers had been cut to ribbons as soon as they had arrived in the town and gathered outside the large bank. Brooks, Sol Cohen and Jody Laker had barely escaped with their lives as the rest of the gang had been slaughtered. For once it had been outlaw blood they had left behind them as they fled empty handed.

Since that time, the three outlaws had kept a low profile and vainly tried to regain their lost reputation. Even wanted dead or alive with a value of $2,000 on their combined heads, it seemed that nobody desired to join their ranks.

The horsemen eased back on their reins and slowed the pace of their exhausted mounts as they rode down the twisting main street.

Apart from the saloon and a small hotel, there were no other lights within Ten Strike. Ben Brooks slowed his mount as they rode past a red brick structure bathed in shadow and pointed to his comrades.

'There it is, boys.' He chuckled.

'Kinda puny, ain't it?' Laker noted as they continued on toward the oil lantern lights.

'Small and sweet, Jody,' Brooks argued. 'Just the way I like my banks. Small and sweet.'

Cohen nodded as he trailed his partners. 'Looks like we can empty that place in a matter of minutes, Ben.'

The three riders drew up outside the saloon. The sound of a tinny piano and a fiddle greeted the trio of outlaws as they dismounted.

Brooks glanced up the street at the hotel. 'We'll bed down in there for the night after we've washed the trail dust out of our throats.'

The three men secured their long leathers and then ducked under the hitching pole and stepped up onto the boardwalk. Brooks glanced up and down the street as the mist trailed along the street like an evil spirit.

His hooded eyes focused on the sheriff's office bathed in darkness. He pulled out a cigar and ripped off its tip with his teeth. He spat and then struck a match on the saloon's porch upright. His gloved hands cupped the flame as he touched it to the end of the cigar.

'Looks like they got themselves a sheriff, boys,' he said through a cloud of cigar smoke. 'We'll have to finish him before we hit the bank.'

'I don't figure he'll give us no trouble.' Laker grinned.

Cohen nodded and pushed the swing doors apart.

The three outlaws entered the saloon and surveyed its interior as they marched across the sawdust covered floor toward the bar counter. Brooks tossed a silver dollar on the surface of the counter.

'Whiskey,' he demanded.

2

The looming trees towered over the stagecoach as it thundered through the darkness and ventured deeper into the vast forest in a bid to reach the distant town of Ten Strike. Yet with every stride of the new team of six horses between the traces, it grew more obvious to the feisty female perched high on the driver's seat that she might have bitten off more than even she could chew. Only faint wisps of moonlight managed to penetrate a path to the rough trail through the dense tree canopy.

A less stubborn person might have quit at sundown but not the ornery Squirrel Sally. She had never been one to admit openly to ever making a mistake but was now beginning to wish that she had listened to Buck Smith back at the sprawling logging town.

The bearded lumberjack had warned her of the danger this seldom used trail posed to the unwary, telling her that it was a treacherous route even in daytime and virtually lethal after dark.

Sally had totally ignored the warnings.

As always she knew better. She had exchanged her exhausted team of horses for a fresh one and set out regardless. After all, she was on a mission to find her beloved Iron Eyes whether he wanted to be found or not.

Her small gloved hands clasped the reins firmly and steered the team further into the blackness. Slowly Sally began to doubt the wisdom of her actions.

She steered the team of horses along the twisting trail across the rugged ground and grimaced at the thought that it would get a lot darker before it grew lighter. Her squinting eyes could hardly see the potholes that threatened to destroy her valiant efforts. The stagecoach jolted unexpectedly as its wheels located a rut in the road.

Sally bit her lip and continued.

The trail was heading toward a massive mountain. Her heart sank as it dawned on her that Buck Smith had not been exaggerating about the dangerous trail.

Sally hated to admit it, even in the privacy of her thoughts, but Buck had been right. This was an unholy trail and no mistake.

At first, the trail which had been carved through the dense forest seemed no better or worse than any other she had travelled but then the sun had set.

Darkness had spread across the untamed terrain like a wildfire. Sally had been quite shocked at how quickly the twisting rough road had succumbed to the enveloping darkness. Black shadows stretched across the team's path as the moonlight vainly tried to reach the ground. Tall trees and a narrow twisting trail were not the ideal travelling companions for a tired young female wrestling with heavy leathers on a high driver's board.

Sally's beautiful eyes strained to see what she was encouraging her horses toward and yet she did not flinch or deviate from her task for even a heartbeat. There was a burning desire inside her that kept her lashing the backs of the powerful animals with her reins.

It was something which she did not fully understand.

Her head was pleading for her to stop but her heart would have none of it. The telegraph wire had said that Iron Eyes was headed for Ten Strike so that was where she was headed.

In her youthful mind, she had no alternative.

Sally knew that she had to find her beloved Iron Eyes as quickly as possible. Something deep inside her pounding heart was screaming to her to find him before it was too late. It was as if his very life depended on her reaching him and yet it made no sense in her young mind.

The trail grew even darker. Sally glanced up at the stars and saw that the tops of the tall trees to either side of the trail were almost touching.

Her journey was going from bad to worse.

As the stagecoach resounded along the eerie trail, Sally became more and more troubled. The coach beneath her rump jolted violently as one of its wheels found another missing chunk on the rough trail.

Sally rocked back and forth as she fought with the long leathers in her hands. The toes of her bare feet were curled around the rim of the driver's box as she reluctantly had to admit to herself that she could not see the ground ahead of the lead horses.

She was driving blind.

She knew that to continue on was suicidal. Sally stood in the box and hauled back on the reins with every last scrap of her dwindling strength. The six horses slowed as she pushed the brake pole forward until it was locked off.

The team stopped as their young mistress looped the long leathers around the brake-pole. Sally exhaled as she attempted to suck some air into her lungs. Her eyes screwed up and looked down upon the resting horses. Steam rose off their backs and drifted into the night air like fleeing phantoms.

Sally sat back down and sighed heavily.

Every sinew in her perfectly formed body ached. It felt as though her muscles had been torn from her bones as she pulled off her gloves and set them down beside her.

Sally was exhausted.

She tossed her head of golden curls back and looked up at the dark sky again. There was a moon up there someplace, she told herself but she had yet to see it.

'That furry Buck was damn right about this trail,' she muttered to herself and then surveyed the surrounding undergrowth. 'I ain't never bin in a place so dark before. One mistake here and I'll wrap this stage around a dozen trees.'

Sally rubbed the dust from her face.

Suddenly the howls of wolves or coyotes rang out through the trees. Her beautiful head jerked to one side. She stared vainly at the black wall of lumber. Was that where the sound had come from, she wondered.

Then another more frightening noise echoed through the forest. It was the echoing growl of a cougar. The painful warning cry of the big cat surrounded the small female sat up high on the top of her stagecoach. Sally swallowed hard but her throat was dry.

'That sounds like a mighty big cat,' she whispered as the team below her rattled their chains nervously.

Her hand reached for her whiskey bottle and dragged it across the driver's board toward her. She lifted it up and pulled its cork. She took a long stiff swallow of the fiery liquor and then patted the cork back into the neck of the bottle.

The whiskey only made her yawn. She placed the bottle back under the seat and then pulled a twisted cigar from her tattered shirt pocket and placed it between her teeth. Her honed hunting instinct told her not to panic. Sally knew only too well that when folks panicked, they made mistakes that could get them dead. The last thing she wanted was to end up in the belly of a cougar.

The horses began to whinny and fight against the brakes of the stage-coach they were chained to. Sally looked down at them and whistled to get their attention.

'Easy, boys,' her voice soothed. 'Ain't no cougar dumb enough to attack the likes of you. That critter's got his eyes on smaller game like me.'

Sally scratched a match across the seat and then lifted it to her cigar. She cupped its flame and sucked in the powerful smoke deep into her lungs. She coughed and then tossed the match at the ground and inhaled again.

The cougar made another daunting growl to her right. Sally lowered her head and blew smoke at her feet as her young mind raced.

Sally saw the barrel of her Winchester propped up in the box. She stretched out her arm and grabbed the rifle and brought it up to her chest. The big cat was still making nerve-shattering growls from the protection of the trees.

She pushed the hand guard down and then pulled it back. A spent casing flew over her shoulder as she eased the weapon's wooden stock into her shoulder and aimed.

Suddenly she unleashed the rifle's fury. A deafening white flash erupted from the barrel of the Winchester and carved a trail through the air in the direction of the big cat.

Another sound came from the trees. It was the sound of a large puma in distress as a bullet came real close to finding its target.

Sally smiled and cocked the smoking rifle again. 'Reckon that feared you.'

She rested the rifle on her lap and sucked hard on the cigar between her teeth. The strong smoke cleared her head as she squinted at the dark trail before her. A few fleeting shafts of filtered moonlight cut through the trees ahead of her.

Not enough to allow even her keen eyesight to see the trail road clearly. She pulled the cigar from her lips and tapped its ash at the ground.

She wondered if it was smarter to continue on or whether it might prove better to crawl into the coach and bed down for the night.

Whichever choice she made, Sally would not be satisfied with it. She inhaled on the cigar again and tried to make up her mind.

The eerie light did little to illuminate the winding road or highlight the potholes in the dirt track trail. Sally knew that if any of her six horses put a hoof into a hole it might prove costly. She could not afford to lose any of the team if she expected to reach her destination.

She chewed on the black weed between her teeth as she pondered the problem and then nearly jumped out of her skin when the loud howling of several wolves filled her ears. Sally grabbed her rifle again, aimed it at the noise and fired two more shots into the darkness. Their unearthly baying stopped for a few moments.

Although tired, Sally was nervous of bedding down in the heart of a terrain filled with wolves and big cats. There was only one way to guarantee survival in land like this and that was to keep moving through it. Staying put was not an option, she told herself.

Then an idea flashed through her tired mind. She snapped her fingers and grinned.

'That's it.' Sally hung the rifle over her shoulder by its rawhide cord, clambered down the side of the stagecoach and ran along the line of horses. She grabbed the mane of one of the lead horses and then climbed up its harness and chains until she was on the powerful animal's back. Her eyes stared at the dusty trail ahead of her from her new position.

Even the darkness could not conceal the smile which covered her joyful face. Sally had a far clearer view of what lay ahead of the horses from her new perch. She grabbed the leathers that were clipped to the horse's bridle and nodded to herself.

'There's more than one way to skin a possum.' She laughed triumphantly. 'C'mon, horse.'

With the blood-curdling noise of timber wolves still ringing around the forest, Sally slapped the neck of the horse and then shook its bridle feverishly. The snorting animal started to move again as the youngster kicked its wide girth with her bare feet.

The stagecoach gathered speed as the rest of the team kept pace with the horse between Sally's thighs.

Within a few precious heartbeats, it was making good time along the shadowy road which she had been told would lead her to Ten Strike and enable her to find the infamous Iron Eyes.

As the stagecoach gathered pace, Sally was totally unaware that she was now heading into the jaws of even more danger.

3

The moonlit clearing sat amid millions of trees bathed in a coating of fresh frost beneath the cloudless sky. The handsome palomino walked across the crisp ground as its master studied the frost like an eagle on a high thermal seeking its next meal. He had trailed the wanted outlaws for close to a hundred miles and only now had all signs of them disappeared from view. The fresh frost was thick on the exposed ground and obliterated the three sets of hoof tracks from his narrowed eyes.

Iron Eyes drew back on his reins and stared across the frosty clearing at the ground which lay before him. He knew that the only town anywhere near this desolate place was a small settlement known by the name of Ten Strike. That was where he intended confronting them.

He looped his long thin leg over the neck of his palomino stallion and slid to the ground. The bounty hunter knelt and brushed the white covering off the ground and studied the three sets of hoof tracks.

They were exactly where he had thought they would be.

A wicked grin fought with the scars on his face as he rose back up to his full height. His bullet coloured eyes stared into the mist which faced him as he pulled both his Navy Colts from his belt and checked their chambers. Both his guns were fully loaded and ready to do his talking for him. Iron Eyes then pushed their barrels down behind his belt buckle and rested his wrists on their jutting ivory grips.

Iron Eyes pulled a half-smoked cigar from his shirt pocket and rammed it between his teeth. He then scratched a match with his thumbnail and lit the twisted black weed. He inhaled the acrid smoke deeply and then tossed the cigar out onto the blanket of white.

He exhaled slowly as thoughts of his long chase filled his mind. The grey smoke hung on the cold air as the bounty hunter thought about the three deadly men he was hunting. Each of them was as deadly as he was with their guns but Iron Eyes was unafraid. Not even death frightened the gaunt bounty hunter, for it had become an old friend.

His bony hand took hold of the reins which hung from the palomino's bridle. He was cold and tired and knew that if he were to face the Brooks gang in his present condition, it might be a costly mistake.

For more days than he cared to recall, the only rest which Iron Eyes had allowed himself had been whilst riding after his unsuspecting prey. For years, the skeletal horseman had learned how to sleep in his saddle as his pure-bred palomino stallion contin-ued to follow the trail of those he hunted.

The haunting figure could sense with

every sinew of his emaciated body that he was gaining on his prey. Like most men who crossed the vast expanses of land in the West, they had bedded down every night around a campfire to sleep unlike the monstrous bounty hunter who trailed them.

He had continued riding while they slept. Iron Eyes knew that he had closed the distance between himself and the wanted bank robbers every single night that they rested. Now he was within spitting distance of the deadly remnants of the once renowned gang, but every muscle and bone in his body ached.

The last three members of the Brooks gang were now so close he could smell them in his flared nostrils. Although he could not see the remote settlement, Iron Eyes was well aware that he was getting close to Ten Strike.

The putrid scent of civilization hung on the cold night air. The hoof tracks were leading right to where Iron Eyes could smell Ten Strike.

Soon the bounty hunter knew that he would catch up with the Brooks gang and administer his own brand of justice. He would do what the law was either unwilling or unable to do.

He would collect the bounty on their collective heads.

Iron Eyes placed a hand on his silver saddle horn and stepped into his stirrup. He rose up from the ground and swung his right leg over his ornate Mexican saddle cantle effortlessly. He poked the toe of his mule-eared boot into his right stirrup and then gathered up his reins. His bony hands held the long leathers as his spurs tapped into the flanks of the magnificent stallion.

The high-shouldered mount started to walk across the hoof tracks as its notorious master leaned back and plucked a whiskey bottle from one of the satchels of his saddlebags. He pulled its cork and finished the last two inches of amber liquor in one long swallow.

The whiskey warmed his innards.

Iron Eyes tossed the bottle over his shoulder and then cracked his reins across the cream coloured tail of the palomino. The horse gathered pace as its ominous master sat like a living ghost astride the stallion.

As the long legs of the mighty horse strode through the frosty mist toward Ten Strike, Iron Eyes propped his painfully lean frame against the saddle cantle.

His mane of long black hair bounced on his wide shoulders as his horrifically scarred face stared blankly ahead with unblinking eyes.

The outlaws did not know it yet but soon Iron Eyes would be upon them. Soon he would have them in his gun sights, daring them to kill him before he killed them.

4

The three deadly outlaws rose around noon and made their way collectively down to the hotel foyer. They did not speak as they filed past the desk and headed toward the glass panelled door. The desk clerk watched the men make their way out into the midday sun with their saddlebags draped over their shoulders. As the door closed behind them, he gave a sigh of relief.

For the first time in a long while, the clerk had actually felt threatened by the unknown men who had rented rooms in the small hotel. He fearfully watched the heavily armed men as they made their way from the front of the hotel and down the street.

The desk clerk mopped his brow nervously and was thankful that they had not booked rooms for more than the one night.

Ben Brooks noticed that Ten Strike seemed no busier than it had done the night before as he led the way along the boardwalk toward the livery stable with Cohen and Laker in his wake. A mere handful of people filled the streets and most of them were of the female variety, going about their daily rituals. Had anyone within the confines of the small town taken the time to study the three strangers, they might have noticed that unlike themselves, the Brooks gang were all heavily armed.

Brooks glanced back at his trailing followers and grinned widely. The hardened bank robber saw no threat in any of the locals. Then his eyes scanned the rooftops of the small settlement.

'What you doing looking up there, Ben?' Laker asked.

'What I should have done before,' Brooks replied as he lowered his stare to what lay before them. 'If I'd checked the roofs back then, maybe most of my gang would still be alive and not rotting in their graves.'

'There was just too many of us, Ben.' Laker shrugged as they continued walking. 'They seen us coming before we seen them.'

Brooks rested a free hand on his gun grip. 'It'll never happen again, Jody. We'll kill them before they get a chance to kill us. Savvy?'

'Yep, I savvy.' Laker grinned.

'This plum is ripe and ready to be plucked, Ben,' Cohen said knowingly. 'Robbing that bank will be easier than taking candy from a baby.'

'Seems that way, Sol,' Brooks agreed.

Laker looked at their leader. 'We gonna do this and high-tail it out of here, Ben? The bank's open. There ain't no sense in delaying.'

'Let's do it, Jody.' Brooks nodded and paused by the livery stable's open doors as Cohen and Laker entered the ramshackle structure to get their mounts. His hooded eyes studied the street carefully and then spotted a middle-aged man making his way toward the sheriff's office. The man was unarmed and far older than Brooks had ever seen anyone else wearing a sheriff's tin star.

The sun glanced off the star like a target waiting to be shot at. The gang leader stroked his whiskered chin and drooled in anticipation. Killing had become a habit he had become addicted to.

Brooks did not take his eyes off the lawman until the elderly man entered his office. Then he heard the sound of their horses behind his shoulders. He turned as Cohen and Laker led the three horses out into the morning sunshine.

Brooks draped his saddlebags over his saddle blanket and then secured them with the leather laces attached to the cantle.

He rested his hands on the saddle and looked straight at his cohorts. 'I just seen the sheriff, boys.'

They both looked at Brooks and noticed the amused grin carved on his face.

'By that look on your face, I reckon that the sheriff ain't exactly a right able looking critter, Ben.' Laker smiled.

'He'll not give us any trouble,' Brooks announced confidently. 'Hell, he wasn't even wearing a gun.'

'Mighty trusting folks in this town, Ben.' Cohen chuckled.

'It'll be the death of them,' Laker added.

'A few of them anyways.' Brooks grinned.

All three of the lethal bank robbers strode away from the livery with their mounts in tow. As they neared the bank, Brooks tossed his reins to Cohen and then left both his men close to the Ten Strike bank building.

Brooks walked past the structure and glanced in through one of its windows. A broader smile filled his face. The bank was exactly as he liked them to be. It had been designed and built long before any of the townsfolk had realized that even this far West there was a breed of deadly men who made their living by robbing such businesses.

Brooks continued on toward the tiny sheriff's office. With each step he readied himself for the execution he was planning.

He knotted the leather lace hanging from his holster around his thigh and then flicked the safety loop off his holstered gun's hammer.

Brooks pulled the brim of his Stetson down over his brow and turned the brass door knob. He swiftly entered the office and moved to where the elderly lawman was preparing his coffee on the wood stove in the corner.

'And what can I do for you?' the sheriff asked without turning toward the outlaw.

Brooks did not answer. The lethal outlaw pulled his gun from its holster and then hammered its metal barrel across the lawman's skull. An eruption of blood flowed from the deep gash as the man crumpled.

Most men are unconscious after one blow from a .45. When the blow is repeated a dozen more times they are no longer unconscious.

They are dead.

Brooks ripped the yellow bandanna from the lawman's neck and cleaned his bloody six-shooter until the cotton was stained in crimson gore. He then holstered the gun and dragged the limp old body into a back room. Brooks threw the lawman in a heap and left him there. A trail of blood led from the stove to the lifeless lawman.

'I bet that spoiled your day, old timer,' Brooks grunted as he closed the door. He quickly glanced around the makeshift office and then saw the office keys on the desk. He snatched them and walked back out onto the board-walk. He locked the office door and started back to where Cohen and Laker waited just beyond the bank. He dropped the keys into a water trough before he reached his men.

'That was quick,' Laker said.

'I didn't even have time to make me a smoke, Ben,' Cohen said as he looked into the face of their leader.

'There'll be plenty of time to make and smoke a cigarette after we rob this little bank,' Brooks said gravely as his hooded eyes watched the street. It was still quiet and devoid of the sort of men that had soured their plans before. 'You get mounted, Sol. You clear the streets if the townsfolk get brave.'

Cohen did not argue. He grabbed his saddle horn, dragged his dishevelled carcass up on to the back of his mount and held the reins of the other horses.

Brooks nodded at Laker. 'C'mon, Jody. Let's see how rich the pickings are in that little ole bank.'

Cohen watched his two cohorts as they slowly made their way toward the bank. He continued to watch the street and hold the reins of their mounts as they slid their guns from their holsters in readiness.

Brooks entered the bank first. Laker followed and stood beside the door. There were just two people inside the Ten Strike Bank and neither of them was armed or alert enough to sense the danger that they faced.

Laker closed the door and rested his shoulder against it as he held his six-shooter and watched for any sign of trouble out in the street.

'What if somebody tries to get in here, Ben?' the outlaw asked his leader.

Brooks shrugged and grinned. 'Let them in, take their money and kill them, Jody.'

One of the men in the bank was elderly with white side whiskers and the other was a long, painfully lean clerk. Neither had heard the words which passed between Brooks and Laker. They still smiled at the strangers.

'I'm Cy Holden,' the older man said as he held out a hand in greeting. 'I own this bank.'

The smiles, which were well-practised, faded from their faces as they realized that these were not new customers but gun-toting bank robbers.

'We're the Brooks gang.' Brooks cocked the hammer of his gun and aimed it at the older man. 'We're here to rob you.'

Holden stared in disbelief and moved backwards to his desk. His eyes flashed between the two outlaws and the terrified young teller.

'You can't do that,' the banker stammered.

'Put all of the cash you got in bags, old timer,' Brooks snarled at the older man. 'Quick or you'll die.'

Holden waved at the teller.

'Fill the bags, Elmer,' he urged the youngster. 'You heard him. Fill the bags with all the money from the cash drawers.'

Ben Brooks pushed the barrel of his six-shooter into the belly of the banker. They stared into one another's eyes. The deadly outlaw looked at the small safe at the back of the bank and then grinned.

'And we want every cent you got hid in that safe as well, old timer,' he added and then pushed the rotund figure across the room.

Flustered, Holden knelt and pulled a key from his coat pocket. He slid its brass length into the lock and turned it. Both men heard the lock inside the metal box as it released.

Brooks grabbed a canvas bag off the banker's desk and tossed it into the face of the kneeling man.

'Now fill this,' he ordered.

Holden did exactly as he was told and filled the bag with large stacks of cash until his watery eyes spotted the handgun at the back of the safe shelf. He handed the canvas sack up to the ruthless outlaw standing above him.

'That's all of it.' He sighed.

Brooks buckled the bag as Holden got to his feet and strode back to the middle of the small room. Sweat rolled freely down the face of the white-whiskered banker as he held the .44 at his side.

For some reason, Holden made the same mistake that so many others had made over the years. He believed that he could stop the determined bank robber with a bullet from the gun in his hand.

Yet unlike the banker, Brooks was no stranger to handling six-shooters. He was also used to fat old men thinking they could take his life before he could react.

From the corner of his eye, Brooks spotted the gun in Holden's shaking hand as the banker raised his arm. The outlaw swung on his heels and fired.

The bank rocked as Brooks unleashed his six-shooter's fury and fired into Holden's wide girth. The gun fell from his grip as the banker staggered forward, toppled over his desk and then slid to the floor clutching his belly.

Brooks kicked the gun into the corner and then glanced at the young teller.

'Unless you want the same, keep filling them bags with all the paper money you got, sonny,' he growled as smoke twisted from the barrel of his gun.

The terrified boy did as he was told and dragged all the bank's paper money from the cash drawers and stuffed it in the canvas bags. Brooks tossed the bag into Laker's hands as the outlaw looked out at the street.

'That shot has made the curious come out onto the street, Ben,' Laker said as he clutched his own weapon to his chest. 'We'd best get out of here before they get brave.'

'You're right, Jody.' Brooks looked down into the watery eyes of the whiskered man as he lay helpless on the floor. Blood was pumping through his fingers.

Brooks glanced at Laker.

'Take the bags off the boy, Jody,' he said.

Laker snatched the canvas bags and then opened the door of the bank as Cohen eased the horses to a standstill outside the red brick building. Laker ran the short distance to his mount and leapt onto its saddle. He hung the bags from his saddle horn and joined Cohen in firing shots at the onlookers.

'C'mon, Ben,' Cohen yelled.

Brooks looked between the two very different men as he walked backwards to the open bank doorway. He was about to turn and follow his partner when he stopped. His thumb cocked his .45.

'Give my regards to Lucifer, Mr Holden,' he rumbled.

With merciless venom, he fired another shot into the wounded old man on the floor and then cocked his hammer again and aimed its smoking barrel at the sobbing youngster. Even though the teller had his arms raised, Brooks still squeezed on his trigger. Red hot fury spewed from his smoking gun barrel for a third time. The bullet hit the thin youngster dead centre like a battering ram.

The teller was knocked off his feet by the impact of the lethal lead. He crashed into the wall behind him and then slid lifelessly to the floor.

A scarlet trail of gore marked the wall.

Brooks ran to his horse and grabbed his reins from Cohen's grasp. He swung his body onto his saddle and turned his wide-eyed horse.

'C'mon, boys,' he yelled out as he fired at the crowd.

Still firing their guns at the astonished townsfolk, the bank robbers spurred and thundered down the street in a cloud of hoof dust. Slowly, when they were convinced that the shooting had stopped, the townsfolk gathered enough courage to move to the bank. Gradually it dawned on the stunned population what had just happened in Ten Strike.

In a mere few minutes of deafening mayhem, their peaceful existence had been brutally changed forever.

The town's savings had gone and so had their collective innocence. The only money that remained in Ten Strike was what they had in their pockets.

Only the acrid stench of gun smoke

and the sight of freshly spilled blood remained in the remote settlement to confirm that the nightmare actually happened. None of those who had witnessed the unexpected outrage seemed capable of knowing what to do next.

All they could do was stare into the confines of the small red brick bank in confused horror at the sickening sight which greeted their naïve eyes.

5

Dust drifted off the side of the rugged mountain into the cloudless blue sky as the stagecoach careered along the blistering sun-baked trail. The fiery female wrestled with the team of matched black horses from her precarious perch as they ascended the steep crumbling road.

Loose gravel fell away from the disintegrating edge of the trail and rained down the mountainside beneath the coach's metal wheel rims.

The rough trail road had not followed the valley floor as Sally had expected during the hours of nightfall. Since sunrise had cast its blazing light across the wooded region, the trail had slowly risen up the side of the steep mountain and fringed its very edge. Without knowing how, Sally had found herself driving the stagecoach along a road barely wider than the vehicle itself.

Terror might have torn her nerves to shreds had she not kept the thought of Iron Eyes branded in her young mind. Sally knew that as long as she kept thinking about him, she had little time to dwell upon the situation she had found herself trapped within.

Sally kept her beautiful eyes focused on the lead horses as they continued to climb the perilous pathway. For the first time since she had taken ownership of the stagecoach, she wished that six sure-footed mules were ascending the dusty trail rather than a team of horses.

As she desperately fought to control the hefty leathers in her gloved hands, Sally began to wonder if she would ever escape from this never ending nightmare.

It took every ounce of her driving skills just to keep the muscular horses on the trail road and stop them from falling to their deaths. Sally refused to fuel her own fear by looking down into the deadly gorge as the wheels of her stagecoach veered ever closer to the cliff edge.

She pressed on defiantly.

There was no alternative.

As dawn broke, Sally had moved back to the driver's seat but was now regretting it. Now there was no escaping the unobstructed view which faced her.

For more than five hours, she had battled her own weariness just to keep the horses and trailing vehicle on the terrifying road. She was hurting from head to toe at the sheer effort of keeping the long vehicle under control.

Battling her increasing exhaustion, Sally somehow managed to guide the stagecoach around an acute bend to where she was faced by a steep drop between walls of countless trees. After what seemed like an eternity, a sense of relief overwhelmed the doggedly determined female.

The sight of the relatively safe route down into an ocean of trees made Sally relax for a moment. She eased back on her reins to slow the team but the sheer weight of the following coach made it virtually impossible for Sally to achieve her goal.

To her surprise the stagecoach was actually gathering speed rather than slowing down.

Frantically, Sally raised her bare foot and pushed the brake pole forward. To her horror there was no resistance and the pole limply fell forward.

Sally held the reins tightly as her mind raced. Her foot pumped the brake pole repeatedly but for the first time since she had acquired the stagecoach, it did not work.

Her wide open eyes stared in horror as the stage gathered pace and hurtled down the steep trail. The horses were galloping in their traces as they tried to outrun the hefty vehicle behind them.

Vainly, Sally hauled back on the long leathers again and tried with all her might to stop her team but she was too exhausted. The stagecoach continued to gain momentum as it thundered down the steep slope.

Desperate to know what was happening, Squirrel Sally leaned over the side of her stagecoach and stared in horror at what she saw. The wooden brake block had been ripped clean off the rear wheel.

She anxiously straightened up as the stagecoach body rocked her petite form back and forth like a rag doll. She was virtually helpless as she held on to the metal baggage rail behind the seat.

Her eyes widened as she stared at the bottom of the trail road that she was careering toward. Again, Sally strained every muscle in her body in an attempt to stop the team of horses' increasingly rapid descent.

Yet no matter how hard she hauled back on the reins, she simply could not slow the vehicle's pace. Time was running out fast and she knew it. The body of the coach shook beneath her split pants. Sally jumped down into the box for protection as the stagecoach reached the foot of the trail. She braced herself as best she could.

As soon as the lathered up team reached level ground, the following coach skidded on its wheel rims. The side of the vehicle slammed heavily into a massive tree. As the coach violently stopped, its team of wide-eyed horses were jerked backwards by the sudden impact as their reins tightened. Only the restraining straps and secure harness chains prevented the terrified animals from severely injuring themselves.

Clouds of dust engulfed the vehicle as the battered and bruised female scrambled up into the box. Dazed and shaken, Sally held onto the lip of the box and stared at her now stationary team. She slowly stood and rubbed her sore head as she tried to gather her wits.

Her grazed fingers pulled the sides of her open shirt together and tied them in a knot under her breasts. She checked her trusty Winchester and then picked up the bottle at her feet. To her relief, it had also survived the sudden impact. She took a long swallow of whiskey and then savoured its fumes as she replaced its cork.

Her shaking hands placed the whiskey bottle on the seat.

Then she rubbed her hand across her face. Sally noticed that the back of her hand was covered in blood. Sally's fingers checked her nose. Although bleeding it did not feel broken.

'Reckon that's lucky,' she sighed cynically.

Mustering the remains of her strength, Sally climbed from the driver's box to the rough ground beside the scarred stagecoach. What little paint the vehicle still boasted had been scraped from its carcass.

She slowly checked each of the horses in turn and then wandered back to the coach. The damage looked far worse than it actually was apart from the missing brake block.

Sally crawled on her belly under the

coach and pulled debris free of the axle. When satisfied she went back into the sunshine and got to her feet.

Her throbbing skull knew that although the brakes had been totally destroyed, the wheels were still somehow attached to the axles. She sighed with relief and then turned to look down the remainder of the trail toward the distant Ten Strike.

The distant town was bathed in sunlight.

'Hell,' she cursed in surprise. 'I'm nearly there.'

Sally stared down into the valley and smiled as she recalled why she had undertaken this arduous trek. This was where she knew she would find the elusive Iron Eyes. This was where her man's trail had led her. She had travelled the better part of a hundred miles to warn the notorious bounty hunter of the strange premonition which haunted her.

'Now I've got you in my sights, Iron Eyes,' Sally mumbled as she lifted her leg and stepped on the rim of the small front wheel below the driver's box. 'You better not be dead or I'll be mighty cantankerous, beloved.'

Even though she was still shaken, Sally climbed back up to the driver's seat and sat down. She lifted the whiskey bottle again and downed a quarter of its contents before forcing the cork back into the bottle's neck.

Now she was ready to tackle the final leg of her long, painful journey. None of her cuts and bruises mattered any longer.

Sally exhaled and stared at Ten Strike from her high vantage spot. It looked so close she felt as though she could reach out and grab it but she knew that the journey was far from over.

The merciless rays of the sun burned her exposed skin as she sat and contemplated the last part of her quest. Then her aching mind thought about the condition of her precious stage-coach. Sally wondered if she would be able to control the powerful six horses without the aid of the vehicles brakes.

The thought troubled her.

Then another even more daunting notion tore at her dazed mind. Sally's eyes surveyed the vehicle below her high seat and wiped the blood off her face.

She was anxious that the stagecoach might not remain intact before she reached Ten Strike. Its recent history had taken a brutal toll on its weathered fabric.

Sally dismissed her concerns and focused on the trail with resolute eyes. It seemed quite level as far as she could tell but a half mile ahead it vanished from view.

Countless trees masked it from her tired eyes.

Would she actually need the missing brakes?

Finding out the answer might prove disastrous, she thought.

Sweat dripped freely from her hair and fell onto her torn pants but the still dazed female did not notice as she continued to study what still lay between Ten Strike and herself.

Ten Strike did not seem that far away to her.

Yet it was too far away to walk. There was only one way for her to reach the settlement and that was to risk her very neck and drive the stagecoach there. She reluctantly picked up the reins and carefully separated them between her gloved hands.

Sally teased the lengths of leathers apart, slapped them down across the backs of the horses and got the team walking again. If she could keep the horses moving at this speed, everything would be fine, she thought.

The stagecoach continued on along the slowly descending trail road and rounded a sharp bend. The tree canopies hung low and the tiny female had to duck under them as the stagecoach slowly moved forward. Then as the horses continued to pull their heavy burden along the leafy glade, a familiar noise filled her ears.

She had heard the distinctive noise before.

It was the sound of flowing water.

Sally pushed the hanging branches aside and guided her team toward the sound. A sound which was growing in intensity with every step of her six horses.

Then the stagecoach cleared the greenery and revealed the one thing she had not expected to see in the dense forest. It was a vision that was beautiful and dangerous in equal parts.

Sally eased back on the reins and slowed the team to a walk as she approached the one thing she had not even considered when she had set out along the unforgiving trail.

A powerful waterfall.

She stared in stunned awe at the impressive and daunting sight which faced her.

The waterfall was at least forty feet high and seemed to be coming straight from a natural fissure in the tree-covered rocks above the trail. Its continuous torrent was hitting the trail road so violently that it filled the small clearing with plumes of water and spray that rose twenty feet up into the sunlight.

Rainbows arched across her path hypnotically as Sally steered the coach across the wet ground toward the ominous vision. She pulled back on her reins and stopped the team twenty yards from where the water was crashing onto the trail road.

A million thoughts raced through her mind. As far as she could tell, this was the only way to reach Ten Strike from the logging road. Sally knew that it was impossible to turn the long stagecoach around in the narrow confines of the trail. She ran her fingers through her damp hair and wondered why the road had taken this course.

Her eyes focused on the wall of water.

'How the hell am I meant to get these animals and stagecoach through that?' Sally muttered to herself as her lovely eyes stared at the battered rocks. Every grain of sand and soil had been washed away from where the waterfall constantly hit the ground. Only bare rock remained at the foot of the flowing torrent. 'Them lumberjacks must have carved out this road during a dry spell. Nobody could have done it at this time of year.'

Sally glanced to see where the volumes of water went after hitting the trail, but all she could make out was a dark hole surrounded by well-nourished plants.

Mist rose up from the devilish hole in the ground. Sally bit her lip and wondered what lay in the depths of that dark abyss. She could hear something like a fast flowing river but the crescendo of falling water was so loud that the young female could not be certain of anything.

She inhaled deeply.

Summoning every scrap of her remaining courage, Sally swallowed hard and carefully picked up the reins and held them in her left hand. Although every inch of her petite form was warning her not to go any further, Sally knew that she had to risk driving her stagecoach through the cascading torrent if she were to reach Ten Strike.

She had to challenge the flowing water's might. There was no other way. Sally had to get to the remote settlement and warn her beloved Iron Eyes about the premonition, which gnawed at her craw, before it was too late.

Sally pulled her bullwhip off the roof of the coach and unfurled its length. She then raised it above her head and expertly cracked it over the heads of the six black horses.

The team bolted like buckshot from a scattergun.

Having tossed the whip aside, Sally rested her feet against the rim of the box and leaned forward with the long leathers in her grip. The six valiant horses obeyed their mistress and galloped blindly into the powerful water as it crashed down onto the rocks before them.

But even the six powerful horses were no match for the waterfall's unyielding might.

From the driver's seat, Sally stared in horror as she witnessed all six horses knocked off the rocky ground and disappear into the abyss. Once the first pair had been washed off the trail the others followed in quick succession. Mist rose up like a ravenous monster and consumed the whinnying horses a mere heartbeat before Sally also felt the unbelievable power of the waterfall hitting her. The unceasing flow of continuous water swept the unfortunate female off the driver's seat. As Sally fell helplessly into the darkness the stage-coach followed her.

Squirrel Sally did not scream.

There was no time.

Within seconds all traces of the beautiful female and her stagecoach were gone from view. They had been swallowed up just like the team of sturdy horses before them and fallen into the watery abyss.

Moments later, only the waterfall and its colourful rainbows remained. It was as though Squirrel Sally and her conveyance had never existed.

6

Ben Brooks drove his bloody spurs harder into his mount's flesh than either of his ruthless companions as they thundered away from Ten Strike. Laker and Cohen followed Brooks along the winding trail into the uncharted forest and did their best to keep pace with their seasoned leader. Dust rose up into the cloudless heavens above the trail as though marking their chosen route for anyone with the guts to follow.

They had ridden more than five miles into what seemed an unoccupied land and not seen anyone either following or ahead of their mounts. Brooks knew that if he followed the seldom travelled trail to the south of Ten Strike, it would eventually lead them to the railhead at Durango.

Everything had gone as Brooks had

said it would. They had achieved their goal and stripped the remote settlement of all its banked cash and made their escape exactly as their leader had planned.

As the tree canopies above them grew closer together and the sunlight no longer bathed the three horsemen in its merciless rays, they slowly began to ease their pace.

There was no more urgency in their spurs. Brooks rode between his lethal men and started to relax for the first time since they had shot up the small settlement.

'How far is it to the railhead, Ben?' Laker asked, pulling his tobacco pouch from his shirt pocket and rolling a cigarette as his mount continued to canter down the twisting rail.

'I can't rightly recall, Jody,' Brooks replied as his eyes scanned the undergrowth which appeared to be closing in on them. 'We ought to reach it before sunup, though.'

Cohen nervously looked all around

them. The hills were covered in trees of every variety, making it virtually impossible for them to see very far.

'I don't like this forest,' he commented as he kept tapping his spurs onto the flanks of his horse. 'An army could be hiding in them trees and we wouldn't be able to see the varmints.'

'There ain't nobody hiding in them trees, Sol,' Laker said as his tongue traced along the gummed paper of his smoke.

'There could be,' Cohen grunted. 'This seems like a perfect place to get bushwhacked.'

'Stop fretting, Sol,' Brooks said. 'When we reach the railhead at Durango, we'll sell these nags and buy us three tickets to Abilene. We got us enough money here to have us a fine old time while I plan our next job.'

The words had barely left his lips when the three riders spotted something fifty yards ahead around a bend in the trail.

Brooks raised an arm and pulled

back on his leathers.

'What is that?' he growled as his cohorts stopped their horses beside him.

Cohen stood in his stirrups and squinted through the filtered sunlight. 'Looks to me like a pinto pony.'

Brooks steadied his skittish mount. 'Yeah, that's what it is. A pinto pony with a rope bridle and a blanket across its back.'

'An Injun blanket by the looks of it.' Laker scratched a match across the top of his saddle horn, raised the flame to the cigarette in his mouth and inhaled the smoke into his lungs. 'And where there's a pinto there's usually an Injun to go with it.'

Brooks drew one of his six-shooters from its holster, cocked its hammer and rested it on his thigh. 'Do either of you boys see an Injun?'

Laker allowed the cigarette smoke to drift from his lips as he carefully watched the tethered pinto pony.

'Nope, I don't see nothing except

that pretty little pony yonder,' he answered before pulling the cigarette from his mouth. 'That Injun is probably off hunting his supper. I don't reckon on him giving us no trouble.'

'Maybe,' Brooks said doubtfully.

'Let's spur hard,' Cohen suggested nervously. 'We'll be long gone down the trail before that Injun gets back to his horse.'

Brooks glared at the pony. 'I don't cotton to Injuns. The only good 'un is a dead 'un.'

Laker tossed what was left of his cigarette at the sand and shook his head.

'Why go looking for trouble, Ben?' he asked.

Brooks did not reply. He tapped his spurs and began approaching the pinto pony. Cohen and Laker followed the hardened outlaw through the rays of sunlight.

When Brooks reached the secured pony, he pulled his leathers to his chest and stopped his horse. He stared at the handsome young colt and started nodding to himself. His eyes focused on the beaded rope reins which were carefully wound around the animal's head and nose.

'Looks like a Kiowa bridle to me, boys,' he remarked.

Cohen edged his mount next to Brooks's horse.

'The Injun don't seem to be around here,' he stated. 'Let's ride for the railhead. C'mon.'

'Sol's right, Ben,' Laker agreed with the nervous Cohen as he steadied his horse. 'We've bin lucky so far. We got the bank money and didn't even get a scratch between us. Let's spur hard and put distance between us and that pinto's master.'

Brooks brooded as he stared at the cocked six-shooter on his thigh. The trouble with killing is that after a short while some men get a taste for blood. Brooks was such a man.

He was about to rage at his cohorts when he heard movement in the brush beside him. His strong left hand jerked on his reins and forced his mount to back away from the pony.

Suddenly the young Kiowa emerged from the undergrowth with a young deer draped across his shoulders. As the brave stepped into the sunlight, he stared in disbelief at the three horsemen that surrounded his black and white pony.

For a moment the Kiowa and the bank robbers just stared at each other. Then the sun glanced across the barrel of the deadly six-gun in Brooks's hand.

The warrior dropped the deer and went to pull his hunting bow from his shoulder. It was a futile gesture with no hope of success.

Brooks smiled as he squeezed his trigger.

His .45 blasted a deafening shot at the young Indian. The bullet lifted the brave off his feet. As the mortally wounded Kiowa landed beside the small deer, Brooks pulled back on his gun hammer again and fired.

Laker swung his horse around and stared at Brooks. Smoke trailed from the barrel of the .45 as the lethal outlaw chuckled to himself.

'Why'd you kill that young buck, Ben?' he shouted.

Brooks rammed the smoking weapon into his holster and then stared at both his travelling companions. The smile had been replaced by the look of a man that wanted to keep killing.

'I killed him cos I wanted to, Jody,' Brooks snarled. 'If you boys got any objections, then you'd best get ready to join that feathered critter in the happy hunting grounds.'

Neither Laker nor Cohen said another word. They were too scared of what Brooks might do next if they opened their mouths again.

Brooks turned his mount and spurred hard.

Even though every instinct in their souls told them otherwise, Laker and Cohen followed the seasoned outlaw. They trailed his hoof dust further south into the dense woodland.

They had to. Brooks was the only one of them that knew how to reach the railhead at Durango.

7

Like a demonic nightmare cast out from the bowels of Hell, the terrifying apparition of the gaunt horseman emerged from the shimmering haze. He tapped his blood soaked spurs into the flesh of the tall stallion and rode deeper into the remote settlement.

The scars of every battle he had ever waged remained carved into his mutilated face. The long limp mane of black hair bounced on his wide, bony shoulders like the wings of a bat seeking its next prey. Everything about the horseman sent out ominous warnings to all who dared look in his direction.

This was no normal being.

He had been created in a mould long since destroyed. A mistake of nature which would never be repeated. For even the Devil could not recreate such a living nightmare.

The infamous Iron Eyes silently guided his handsome mount into the strange unknown town. It was a place he had never visited before. His small bullet coloured eyes studied the ground and the hoof tracks which had brought him to Ten Strike. His hunting prowess was still as honed as ever, making him the most lethal of all those who still practised his unwholesome profession. As the sand grew more and more churned up, Iron Eyes raised his eyes and concentrated on the structures before him.

He knew that the outlaws he sought had ridden this way to inflict their own kind of poison upon fresh victims. Soon he would stop them the only way he knew how.

Iron Eyes would capture and then kill them.

There was no other way. Society had branded them and placed a bounty on their heads. The law wanted them dead and that was good enough for the gaunt horseman.

His flared nostrils caught a familiar scent on the dry air which drifted along through the streets of Ten Strike. It was the scent of freshly killed people.

The sickening smell of death lingered in Ten Strike as the sound of his approaching hoof beats echoed off the town's weathered buildings.

Few men would have detected the fresh stench of decay but Iron Eyes was no ordinary man. He was and had always been a hunter who had once used his unmatched skill to track and kill animals for their meat and furs. When he realized that his ability could bring richer rewards if he hunted wanted outlaws instead, Iron Eyes had become legendary.

Masked by the heat haze, Iron Eyes continued to steer the stallion further into the heart of the still stunned township like a silent corpse.

Iron Eyes tilted his head and listened to the people he had yet to spy through the whirlpools of molten air. He did not slow or alter his mount's pace. He simply sat astride the ornate Mexican saddle and allowed the palomino to continue into the middle of Ten Strike.

He pushed the tails of his trail coat back to reveal his deadly pair of Navy Colts. The blue steel gun grips poked out from behind his belt buckle like the tusks of a wild boar. They were ready for action.

Iron Eyes was also ready.

Fear swept through the hearts of every living soul in Ten Strike like a wildfire. They listened fearfully to the horse's hoofs pounding.

The Devil's heartbeats could not have chilled them more.

Every man, woman and child looked toward the nerve shattering noise which grew louder and louder. Those who had started to remove the bodies from the bank and sheriff's office suddenly stopped. They dropped their blood-soaked cargo and backed away from the noise.

A million thoughts raced through their minds. Were the killers returning to kill even more of them? Maybe a new killer was riding in Ten Strike to mop up what was left of their collective money.

So many questions and so few answers.

Iron Eyes emerged through the haze. The blinding sunlight danced off his mount's silver livery as he raised a bony hand to shield his eyes from the merciless rays.

Then he caught a fleeting glimpse of the town's inhabitants.

His red raw eyes surveyed the fearful townsfolk from behind the limp strands of long black hair which hung before his face.

As Iron Eyes saw them, they also saw him. A collective gasp of horror swept through the townsfolk as one by one they glimpsed his brutalized features.

Few creatures had ever survived such horrific injuries but the bounty hunter did not die easy. Every battle he had ever waged was carved into his scarred face. His mutilated flesh appeared to have been stretched over his skull by someone who had never seen what a human head actually looked like.

None of them had ever witnessed anything that remotely looked like Iron Eyes before. After attempting to clean up the sickening mess they had found in both the bank as well as the sheriff's office, their attention was gripped by the unexpected appearance of Iron Eyes.

They panicked at the sight of the unholy horseman.

Undaunted, Iron Eyes did not move a muscle as every one of the crowd scattered from the street. He drove his spurs back into the flesh of the magnificent stallion and watched them flee in a bid to find sanctuary.

The infamous horseman raised a busted eyebrow. He reached back to one of the satchels of his saddlebags and pulled out his last whiskey bottle and dragged its cork free with his teeth. He spat the cork at the sand and raised the bottle neck to his scarred lips.

Iron Eyes swallowed the last inch of fiery liquor and then tossed the empty vessel over his wide, bony shoulder.

The watchful onlookers trembled and vainly waited for the ominous stranger to unleash his lethal lead and start killing, but Iron Eyes did not do anything except guide his high-shouldered stallion into the centre of Ten Strike.

They had never seen anything like the bloodstained scarecrow before. A mixture of terror and curiosity pumped through their veins at the sight of the deathly Iron Eyes.

Every one of them wanted to run away from the monstrous rider but they could not move a muscle. However horrific his appearance, they could do nothing except watch as Iron Eyes rode silently toward them.

They remained secreted in their hiding places and were unable to take their eyes off him as the palomino stallion advanced.

Iron Eyes had the same seductive allure of a public hanging. Onlookers could not look away from his emaciated carcass in the same way that they would watch a man with a noose around his neck and wait for him to drop through the gallows trap door.

It had only been two hours since the Brooks gang had galloped out of the small settlement and now it seemed that one of them was returning to add more notches to his gun grips.

But none of the Brooks gang had resembled anything like Iron Eyes.

His hidden audience watched the ghostlike rider as his squinting eyes darted from one terrified face to another. Then he caught a whiff of the sickening smell again.

Iron Eyes knew that he was close to the bodies that were slowly decomposing in the afternoon heat. He spurred the powerful stallion and increased its speed as his eyes searched the buildings to both sides of the street.

His long hair bounced on his wide

shoulders like wings from his skeletal frame.

The beleaguered horseman was in total contrast to his magnificent mount. The stallion was adorned in silver trimmings and strode as only a thoroughbred could. Iron Eyes resembled a dead body strapped onto its glorious back. Yet however mismatched horse and rider were, they seemed in perfect harmony as they neared the blood-stained bank.

Iron Eyes abruptly tugged back on his reins and stopped the tall palomino stallion beside the small red brick structure. He turned his head and stared at the wide open door of the bank knowingly. The notorious bounty hunter looped his leg over the creamy mane of his mount and slid to the ground.

He rested his wrists on the grips of his Navy Colts as they jutted out from behind his belt buckle. Iron Eyes knew the hidden townsfolk were watching his every move. He placed a thin cigar between his razor sharp teeth as his icy stare darted to every one of his concealed observers.

He pulled a match from his shirt pocket, scratched its red tip with his thumbnail and lit the cigar. Smoke filled his lungs as he dropped his head and stared at the fragrant bank before him.

Iron Eyes led the tall-shouldered horse to a hitching rail and secured his long leathers. He could smell the gun smoke still harbouring within the bank as he slowly approached the open doorway.

His eyes narrowed as he looked inside the blood-splattered building. The afternoon heat had already started to cause the bodies to decay. He rubbed his nose in a vain bid to rid his nostrils of the stench as he turned away from the recent slayings.

The legendary bounty hunter straightened up to his full height and looked around the street.

He sensed that at least a hundred or more eyes were watching his every move. Iron Eyes stepped back to the horse, pulled its reins free of the pole and started across the sand toward the closest structure.

His eyes glanced at the facade nailed across the porch overhang as he walked toward the weathered structure. The Hogleg Saloon had the kind of scent he preferred to the one he had just inhaled.

Stale liquor and a variety of bodily fluids mixed in a heap of sawdust were always better than the stench of death. Even to the hardened bounty hunter.

Like a living corpse, Iron Eyes continued slowly across the sun-baked street toward the saloon. He did not pause until he reached a trough where he allowed his magnificent horse to drink as he tied the animal's reins to the saloon upright.

Once again, Iron Eyes looked all around him. He saw heads ducking for cover and then he stepped up onto the boardwalk and pushed the saloon swing doors inward.

Iron Eyes entered the Hogleg like a bad nightmare. He pulled the cigar from his lips and allowed the smoke to drift through his teeth.

It was the first time that he had entered a saloon in the middle of day only to find it deserted. His eyes focused on a line of whiskey bottles on a shelf in front of a rectangular mirror behind the long bar counter.

Iron Eyes pushed the cigar between his teeth and nodded to himself.

'That's what I'm looking for,' he growled.

His painfully thin legs took him across the sawdust covered floor to the bar counter where he paused and studied the interior of the long room more carefully. Apart from colourful tin plate advertisements upon its walls, the Hogleg resembled a hundred other saloons he had visited over the years.

There was one difference, though. One which seemed curious to the gruesome figure. The Hogleg was far neater than the rest of the saloons he had frequented.

Iron Eyes wondered why.

It was a question which he would soon learn the answer to.

He stared over the counter into the freshly polished mirror and watched the reflection. He could see the street clearly and the nervous people that had trailed him to the saloon. A wry grin etched his horrific features as he stared at the reflections of men, women and children watching him.

They were totally oblivious to the fact that his cruel eyes were watching them like an eagle on a warm thermal studies its prey.

Iron Eyes lifted his left boot and rested it on the brass rail which ran the length of the bar counter. He plucked the spent cigar from his mouth and dropped it into a spittoon. It hissed before sending up a puff of smoke from the middle of the brass vessel.

Iron Eyes lifted his thin frame up off the floorboards and reached across the counter to the shelf. His bony fingers grabbed the neck of a whiskey bottle and pulled it to him. His eyes continued to watch his naive observers as his teeth pulled the cork from its neck.

He took a long swig.

The fiery liquor burned a trail down his dry throat. It felt good. Mighty good. Iron Eyes lowered the bottle and then swiftly swung around on his heels to face the many eyes that were watching him.

They were like jack rabbits. Frozen to the spot by his impenetrable stare.

He leaned back against the counter, raised the bottle and called at the numerous onlookers.

'Any of you critters need a drink?' he called. 'I'm buying.'

His words seemed to hit a few of the more thirsty folks like well-aimed bullets. The unyielding sun made it easy to lure them into the saloon. Slowly the room was filling with more and more of the townsfolk.

Thirst and the offer of free drinks

swiftly outweighed any fears they might have had about the intentions of the tall gaunt stranger.

Iron Eyes lowered his head so that his long black hair fell over his face. The bounty hunter turned back to face the wall mirror again as the saloon gradually filled with the curious crowd.

A man in a white apron made his way around the bar counter and started placing glasses on top of its damp surface.

Iron Eyes could spot a bartender at a hundred paces. He reached into his trail coat pocket and searched amid the dozens of loose bullets until he located a coin. He pulled out a golden eagle and tossed it into the man's hands.

'Drinks for everybody, barkeep,' he drawled as he put the neck of the bottle to his lips again and took two more swallows.

The bartender picked up a bottle of whiskey and pulled its cork. He then expertly filled the line of glasses with the amber liquor.

'You got a name, stranger?' the bartender asked as he poured whiskey at a speed which the bounty hunter admired. 'We ain't seen you in these parts before.'

'I ain't bin in these parts before,' Iron Eyes said.

'But what do they call you?' the bartender repeated.

Iron Eyes lifted his head and shook the limp hair off his dehumanized face. A mutual gasp filled the saloon as they saw the terrible scars his face bore.

'They call me Iron Eyes,' he answered.

The bartender had the best view of the bounty hunter's maimed features. He swallowed hard and then continued to fill and refill the glasses of the rest of his customers.

'I've heard tales about you,' the bartender said as he emptied the last drops of the whiskey bottle into a glass. 'I thought you was just a tall story.'

'I'm tall OK, barkeep,' Iron Eyes said dryly as he pulled another long thin cigar from his coat pocket and pushed it into the corner of his mouth. 'But I ain't no made up story.'

'I can see that,' the bartender said as he plucked another whiskey bottle off the shelf behind him and removed its cork before continuing his serving duties.

A genial old man standing next to the bounty hunter produced a match and ignited it with his thumbnail. He offered it to Iron Eyes.

'Allow me, Iron Eyes,' he said politely.

Iron Eyes leaned forward, sucked the flame into the long black weed and nodded.

'Much obliged,' he said as smoke filtered through his teeth. His eyes darted around the saloon at the faces of the terrified people inside the saloon.

'My name's Sam Parker,' the old timer said before blowing out the match's flame and dropping the spent sliver of wood into a spittoon. 'Sorry we seemed a trifle nervous when you rode in, son.'

'Most of you still look a tad troubled, Sam,' Iron Eyes said as he pulled the cigar from his scarred lips. 'I usually get folks scared but not as bad as you all were.'

'It wasn't you we was scared of,' Sam explained. 'We thought you might be one of the gang that killed the sheriff and bankers two hours back.'

Iron Eyes levelled his eyes at the old timer.

'They killed the sheriff as well?' he asked.

Everyone within the saloon nodded at the same time.

'They sure did,' Sam continued. 'They spent the night in the hotel, then the bastards killed the sheriff and then slaughtered old man Holden and his boy in the bank.'

Iron Eyes took a swig from his bottle. As the whiskey travelled down into his innards, the bounty hunter thought about the men he was chasing. They seemed to have a lot more vigour than he had imagined.

'Three outlaws?' he checked.

'Yep, three outlaws,' someone behind his wide shoulders confirmed. 'Meanest galoots to ever ride into Ten Strike, mister. This is a peaceful town. We ain't never had trouble like this before.'

Iron Eyes frowned and then noticed that not one of the men in the Hogleg was armed. It seemed strange to the bounty hunter.

'Ain't none of you got a gun?' he questioned.

'We ain't ever needed any guns, Iron Eyes,' the bartender said as he continued to fill whiskey glasses. 'Until today, that is.'

The bounty hunter pulled the cigar from his mouth and tapped its ash onto the floor.

'I'm hunting for three outlaws led by a varmint named Ben Brooks,' he explained. 'I've trailed them for a hundred miles or more. Their hoof tracks led right to this town. Reckon I nearly caught up with them.'

'They're vicious, Iron Eyes,' Parker said wearily. 'Really vicious.'

A smile etched a trail across the bounty hunter's scarred face as he pushed the cigar between his teeth. 'They ain't the only ones, Sam.'

'If you head on out by the south road you can catch them, Iron Eyes.' The bartender pointed. 'Them outlaws ain't got more than two hours' lead on you.'

'You could catch them before sundown,' another voice said.

Iron Eyes shook his head and shrugged.

'I'm tuckered out. I need some shut eye before I go squaring up to them varmints. My horse is tired as well. We ain't stopped since we started out after the Brooks gang.'

Parker looked up at the coarsened face. 'You telling us that you've ridden for a hundred miles without resting up?'

Iron Eyes puffed on the black cigar and nodded. 'Yep, I don't like sleeping out under the stars if I can avoid it. I do my sleeping in hotel beds.'

'How come?'

'I don't hanker for wild critters sinking their fangs in me,' he admitted. 'Nope, I do my sleeping in hotel rooms on real beds.'

The old timer took the bounty hunter's sleeve.

'Them outlaws took every penny from the bank, Iron Eyes,' he said seriously. 'Ten Strike is a small town and we can't afford to lose that much money. We need you to get our savings back, son.'

Iron Eyes looked down through a cloud of cigar smoke.

'Are you trying to hire me, Sam?' he asked.

The old man looked around the faces of his neighbours and then returned his eyes to the tall man. He gave a nod of his head.

'Yep, I'm trying to hire you, son,' he said nervously. 'We need that money back or Ten Strike will be just another ghost town. It's our life savings.'

Iron Eyes was thoughtful. 'After I've had a long sleep in the hotel yonder, I might consider it.'

'We'll give you a share of whatever you recover,' the bartender piped up amid a crowd of nodding heads.

'How much?' Iron Eyes wondered.

'I reckon a quarter would be fair,' Sam offered.

'And free whiskey?' the emaciated bounty hunter said.

'Deal.' Sam nodded.

Iron Eyes stared around the faces in the room. He nodded and then started back toward the swing doors. As the emaciated bounty hunter reached them, he paused and looked over his wide shoulder.

'One of you can take my horse down to the livery and get him bedded down. I'll probably set out after nightfall,' he said as he placed a bony hand on the top of the doors. 'I'm going to the hotel and getting me some shuteye.'

Sam walked after the bounty hunter.

'You will help us, won't you?' he repeated. 'I'm begging you for the rest of us. We'll be ruined if them outlaws get away with our life savings, Iron Eyes.'

A smile etched his scarred face. He stepped to the edge of the boardwalk and cast his eyes up at the hills due south of the town. He glanced at Parker for a moment.

'There was one thing you forgot to mention, Sam,' Iron Eyes drawled as he looked out into the blazing sunlight. 'By my reckoning it's a mighty important detail.'

'And what was it I forgot to tell you, Iron Eyes?' Parker asked.

The bounty hunter placed the whiskey bottle in one of his deep pockets and raised an eyebrow. 'You said the Brooks gang headed south after they done their robbing and killing. Right?'

Every one of the townsfolk was staring at the tall emaciated bounty hunter as he rested a bony hand on the porch upright thoughtfully and awaited an answer.

'So what if they rode south?' Parker asked.

Iron Eyes lifted his arm and pointed a bony digit at the trees south of the remote settlement. Ominous black smoke was trailing up into the cloudless blue sky from deep within the depths of the trees. He tilted his head and pushed his long hair from his skeletal features.

'Seems to me that Ten Strike has got some neighbours down yonder, Sam,' he noted before spitting his cigar at the sandy ground. 'They're the feathered type and if my reading of them smoke signals is right, they're real angry about something.'

'That's just a forest fire,' someone in the crowd remarked. 'We get lots of them this time of year.'

'Damn smart forest fire,' Iron Eyes argued. 'It says that three white riders just killed one of their young bucks. They ain't too pleased about it.'

'Is that what it says?' Parker loosened

his collar. 'We ain't ever had no trouble with them Injuns. That's why we never said nothing about them.'

Iron Eyes gave a muted chuckle.

'I hope you're right, Sam,' he said. 'Trouble is, I've never met an Injun yet that didn't want to kill me. Don't know why but they don't cotton to me.'

Parker edged closer to the thin tall bounty hunter.

'And what do you do when they try to kill you?' he ventured.

There was a cold silence and then Iron Eyes shrugged.

'I kill anyone that's trying to kill me, Sam.' He exhaled. 'They've come close a few times to finishing me over the years. I didn't always look like this.'

'Is that how you came to be so scarred?' Parker asked the brooding bounty hunter.

'Partly.' Iron Eyes smiled as best as his mutilated face would allow and eased himself away from the wooden upright. He glanced at the faces of the men and women briefly and then turned away. 'A lot of white varmints added to my tally of scars, Sam. Not just Injuns.'

Sam Parker could see his fellow townspeople urging him forward to confirm that the bounty hunter was going to try and retrieve their life savings from the ruthless Brooks gang.

'Tell me, Iron Eyes. You still willing to try and get our money back for us?' Parker asked sheepishly as the bounty hunter started to head toward the hotel.

Iron Eyes glanced over his shoulder and stared through his hair at the rotund man.

'Sure, I'll get your savings back. After all, I've gotta go after them bank robbers to collect the bounty on their heads, Sam,' he said dryly. 'Their hoof tracks lead south so that's where I'm headed. I'll trail them hombres even if it costs me my scalp.'

'That's mighty brave.'

'Being brave and being stupid are kinfolk from the same litter, Sam.' Iron Eyes stepped down on to the sand.

'Tend my horse and get him watered and fed.'

They watched as the gaunt man continued down the street and entered the hotel. Sam Parker pushed his way through the crowd back to the bar and held his empty glass out.

The bartender filled the glass with whiskey.

'You kinda shied away from telling Iron Eyes the whole truth there, Sam,' he said to the older man as he watched Parker down the fiery liquor. 'We all know that them Kiowa are real ornery when they're riled.'

'And if Iron Eyes read them smoke signals right, they're mighty riled.' A stammering voice piped up from within the crowd.

Parker exhaled.

'I got me a feeling that Iron Eyes gets a tad ornery himself when he's riled up.' He sighed as the bartender refilled his glass. 'I wouldn't wanna be either a bank robber or a Kiowa when that sorrowful looking critter heads south.'

The bartender placed a toothpick in his mouth and rotated it around his teeth.

'I heard tell that Iron Eyes can't be killed, Sam. They say he's already dead but don't know it. They say he's a ghost that can't get into either Heaven or Hell. He's trapped here with us living folks.'

Parker lifted the whiskey glass to his lips and poured its contents down his throat as the bartender's words tormented his mind.

'If that's true,' he gulped, 'we just hired ourselves a dead man to go up against a pack of vicious outlaws and a bunch of vengeful Injuns.'

Even though the Hogleg saloon was full to overflowing, it suddenly fell silent as they considered the odds of anyone actually surviving either breed of adversary.

Maybe only a dead man could, they eventually reasoned.

8

Darkness enveloped the dense forested hills to the south of Ten Strike as the bank robbers continued to spur their mounts deeper into the vast unknown. The three ruthless horsemen had ridden until the sun eventually set before they drew rein and stopped their lathered up mounts. They had not seen the signal smoke but they knew that the brutal slaying of the lone Kiowa brave had not gone unnoticed by the rest of the slain warrior's kinsmen.

The war drums told them that. They echoed through the tree-covered hills like the beating of countless hearts. Neither of the bank robbers could tell where the drums were coming from, all they knew for sure was that they seemed to be everywhere.

Ben Brooks dismounted first and held on to his leathers tightly as his eyes scanned the surrounding trees for any sign of more Indians.

Sol Cohen slid silently from his saddle and bit his lip as he pulled his weary horse up to the side of the brooding Brooks.

'You shouldn't have killed that Injun, Ben,' Cohen said nervously as the noise of the incessant drums drilled into his skull. 'We could have just beat the tar out of him and left him back there. Killing that young buck was just plumb stupid.'

Brooks grabbed the shirt collar of Cohen and dragged him closer. Even the darkness could not hide the fury burning in his eyes as the gang leader snorted into his cohort's face.

'I killed that young buck, Sol,' Brooks growled, 'because he was in our way. I killed him just like I'll kill you if you ever dare to question me again.'

Jody Laker steered his horse right up to his partners and let his snorting mount draw their attention.

Brooks glanced up at Laker and was about to rage at him when he noticed that the young outlaw was staring through the twilight at something else.

He released Cohen and squinted. 'What you see, Jody?'

'I'm looking yonder, Ben.' Laker pointed up the rise where the trees were entangled. 'Do you see it?'

Brooks took a step forward. 'All I see is moonlit trees and shadow. What the hell do you see?'

Cohen began to nod. 'I see something up there as well, Ben. Whatever it is, I don't reckon on it being sociable.'

Brooks gritted his teeth. He was angry.

Angry at the fact that he had not figured there might be Indians in this part of the territory to hamper their escape from Ten Strike. Angry that he had lost his temper and killed one of them and angrier that the constant sound of war drums was slowly driving him out of his mind.

'I don't see nothing,' he insisted.

'There ain't nothing there. You boys are seeing things.'

Laker tapped his spurs and allowed his tired horse to step between his partners. He leaned over the money bags and then dismounted.

'I don't see things that ain't there, Ben,' he said. 'I see trouble and I see feathers.'

Brooks looked at Laker and then returned his eyes to the eerie half-light. He was about to start arguing again when he too saw something move beyond the wall of trees.

Brooks turned to his alert young cohort. 'You're right, Jody. There is something up yonder and if your eyes reckon it's Injuns, then I ain't gonna disagree.'

'What'll we do, Ben?' Cohen was nervous as he turned on his heels and studied the trees which surrounded them. 'We can't fend off a whole tribe of Injuns. We ain't got the ammunition.'

'Our horses are spent, Ben,' Laker added as he kept his eyes glued on the distant movement as his hand rested on one of his six-shooters. 'If we don't get ourselves fresh horse flesh, we'll never get out of this forest.'

'You're both right, boys,' Brooks admitted. 'We ain't got enough bullets and these horses are tuckered.'

Cohen moved closer to Brooks. 'We should leave the trail and head into the woods. We're sitting ducks out here.'

Brooks rubbed his neck. 'I don't recall any Injuns in these parts the last time I rode this way. I just don't understand where they come from.'

Laker held on to his horse's bridle. 'Maybe they got themselves kicked off their homeland like all them other tribes I heard tell about. Maybe the government brought them here.'

'However they got here, the fact is that they're here,' Cohen said bluntly. 'And they're gonna scalp us the first chance they get.'

'That's crazy talk,' Laker said.

The beating drums continued to echo off the trees all around them. It felt as though they were closing in on the outlaws.

'Sol's right, Jody,' Brooks said as he glanced around the countless shadows which encircled them. 'I let my hatred of Injuns cloud my judgement back there. I seen that young buck and just shot him without thinking. Now we got the whole tribe festering to skin us alive, boys.'

Neither Cohen nor Laker had ever heard Brooks admit to making a mistake before. It unnerved them to see their leader so uncertain.

'Which way is the trail out of these hills, Ben?' Laker asked. 'Which way was you intending to lead us away from that little town back there?'

Brooks inhaled deeply and aimed his finger to their left.

'The trail leads thataway,' he said. 'By my figuring, if we cut up through them trees opposite and head straight and true, we should be able to rejoin the trail in about two miles.'

'And that would mean we don't have

to tangle with them critters hid down yonder.' Cohen grinned.

'I don't cotton to trying to fight a bunch of Injuns in the open.'

Brooks grabbed his saddle horn and stepped into his stirrup. He hoisted his weary body up and onto his saddle, and gathered up his leathers.

Laker swung himself onto his saddle and pulled his horse's head back. As he steadied the tired animal, Cohen clambered back onto his own mount.

'Lead the way, Ben,' Laker said. 'You know the trail off this tree-covered mountain. You lead and me and Sol will follow.'

Brooks led the two outlaws off the dusty trail and into the dense trees. He continued to spur as they attempted to out flank their feathered foes.

Yet no matter how far they journeyed, the sound of pounding war drums grew no fainter.

9

Moonlight filled the sparse hotel room and woke Iron Eyes from his deep sleep. He was instantly aware that he had slept through the hot afternoon hours of blistering sunlight and awoke as soon as darkness entered the room. The emaciated man sat up and swung his feet onto the floorboards. He dragged his boots on and then pulled the large Bowie knife out of the boards where it had been embedded before he had slept. He slid the blood-stained blade into the neck of the right boot and stared at the window.

The light of the moon crossed from the window to his boots as Iron Eyes allowed his mind to awake. After a few moments he stood up and stretched the knots in his painfully lean frame free. He walked to the window and stared down into the street as an old man dutifully lit each of the street lights with a flame on a long pole.

Iron Eyes picked his whiskey bottle off the wooden sill of the window and drained its contents. His innards warmed up as he picked up his ragged trail coat and put it on.

The bounty hunter had fallen asleep as soon as his head had touched the solitary pillow on the wide bed. He picked up his spurs and attached them to his boots and then looked down at the bed sheets.

The shape of his thin body was carved into the surface of the bed. His pair of matched Navy Colts rested to either side of the impression where he had left them.

Iron Eyes reached across the bed and picked both deadly weapons up and then pushed them into the deep coat pockets to either side of his hips. The sound of the guns mixing with the countless loose bullets in his pockets filled the room as the tall bounty hunter turned and strode to the room door.

His bony left hand released the bolt and then he stepped out onto the landing. By the time he had reached the staircase he was totally awake.

The hotel clerk looked up from his newspaper when the sound of Iron Eyes's spurs filled the lobby. His face could not disguise the fear which rippled through his body at the sight of the hideous bounty hunter descending the steps.

Iron Eyes looked through the hair which hung over his face at the terrified man behind the desk. He continued walking until the boardwalk was beneath his boot leather.

Only then did he stop and look all around.

The street lights glowed like fireflies. The small town was quiet apart from the saloon. He turned his wide shoulders and started down toward the Hogleg as his eyes surveyed the street as they always did.

He reached the saloon and looked

over the swing doors into its smoke-filled interior. Sam Parker was sat with a gathering of equally old men at a card table as he noticed the bounty hunter.

He rose with Iron Eyes's saddle bags and rushed to the swing doors. They rocked on their hinges as the breathless man handed the bags to the thin figure.

'I put four bottles of rye in these bags for you, Iron Eyes,' Sam said as the bounty hunter accepted the bags and swung them on to his shoulder. The satchels balanced to either side of his lean frame.

'Obliged.' Iron Eyes nodded as he began to walk along the boardwalk with the smaller man at his side toward the livery stable. 'How long have I bin up in that room?'

'Only a few hours,' Sam answered. 'Four at best.'

Iron Eyes patted his clothing and then fished out a long black cigar. He put it between his teeth and then ignited a match with his thumbnail. As smoke filled his lungs, he tossed the match at the sand and stepped down from the boardwalk to cross toward the stable.

'They went south?' Iron Eyes checked through a cloud of smoke.

Parker nodded. 'That's right.'

As both men reached the open doors of the livery, Iron Eyes turned and squinted to the south of Ten Strike. He scratched his jaw.

'With any luck them Kiowa will have killed the varmints already, Sam,' he drawled. 'I was intending on collecting the bounty on their sorrowful hides but there might not be too much left when them Injuns are finished with them.'

A nervous smile lit up Parker's face. 'Do you reckon?'

Iron Eyes shrugged. 'Nope. Just wishful thinking on my part, Sam. Ben Brooks and his boys are too ornery to make my job that easy.'

Parker touched Iron Eyes's arm. 'You won't forget about the money, will you? We sorely need that money, son.'

'If I find the bank money I'll bring it back.'

Iron Eyes continued on into the livery stable and glanced at the blacksmith. The man did not have to be told that the bounty hunter had come for his horse.

Both Parker and the tall bounty hunter watched as the blacksmith led the palomino stallion out of a stall and began to saddle the high-shouldered animal.

'How are you gonna catch them bank robbers?' Parker asked Iron Eyes. 'Have you got yourself a plan?'

'I got me a plan OK.' Iron Eyes snorted as smoke drifted from between his teeth. 'A real good plan, Sam.'

Parker looked up at the strange man as he watched his horse being readied.

'What's your plan?' he asked.

Iron Eyes looked down at Parker through his hair. He tilted his head and then walked to where the magnificent stallion stood in its finery. The bounty hunter did not speak as he placed his saddlebags across the back of the mount and secured them to the ornate cantle.

As the blacksmith walked back to his supper next to the forge, Parker approached the bounty hunter as Iron Eyes stepped into his stirrup and mounted the animal in one fluid action.

'You said you had a plan, son.' Parker pressed the expressionless horseman. 'What is it?'

Iron Eyes glanced down at Parker. A cruel grin came to his scarred lips as his bony hands gathered up his long leathers in readiness.

'I'm gonna kill them, Sam,' he said. 'Simple as that.'

Sam Parker had no time to ask any more questions of the gaunt horseman. Iron Eyes tapped his spurs into the flanks of the stallion and steered it out into the lantern lit street. As the older man rushed to the barn doors, all he could see was the awesome figure riding south with his long hair beating on his shoulders.

Parker stopped at the sight. He slowly turned and made his way back into the vast livery.

'What you staring at, Sam?' the blacksmith asked as he lifted his tin plate and looked at his supper. 'You look like you just seen a ghost.'

'Maybe I have, Jeb,' Parker stammered. 'Maybe I just have.'

'What you mean?' the blacksmith asked as he scooped a spoonful of food up and filled his mouth.

Nervously, Parker removed his hat, mopped his brow, turned and looked at the blacksmith beside the forge. He was visibly shaking as he approached his friend.

'I just noticed something kinda scary about Iron Eyes, Jeb,' he said fearfully. 'That critter's long dark hair looks like the wings of a bat when he's riding.'

The blacksmith nodded.

'That ugly critter ain't human, Sam,' he said. 'No living man could look that dead.'

Parker could not disagree.

10

With the sound of ominous war drums ringing in their ears, the three depraved horsemen steered their mounts through the trees and across the rough ground back toward the trail which their leader insisted led to the Durango railhead. The Brooks gang had cut a path through the dense forest to avoid the Kiowa braves they feared might attack them, yet the sound of drumming had followed them every step of the way. The outlaws drove their mounts down toward the moonlit road and drew rein as soon as the horses reached the rugged pathway.

They were all bleeding from cuts inflicted by untamed brambles entangled between the countless trees. None of them had escaped the sharp thorns.

Brooks gritted his teeth and dragged a gun from its holster angrily. He swung his horse around as his eyes vainly sought out the Kiowa warriors that continued to beat their drums in warning of what was yet to come.

'How the hell can we still hear them blasted drums?' he snarled as he desperately sought something to shoot at. 'We must have ridden these nags miles through them trees and yet them drums are still dogging us.'

Cohen held his own horse in check as he too looked at every dark shadow. 'It must be that the sound is echoing off these trees, Ben. I bet that none of them Injuns are within two miles of us.'

'I don't buy that, Sol,' Brooks grunted. 'They're close, I tell you. So close I can smell them.'

Laker patted the two money bags which hung from his saddle horn. Although younger than both of his cohorts, Laker was in many ways less volatile.

Brooks eased his horse up to Laker's mount.

'What do you reckon, Jody?' he

asked. 'How'd you figure it, boy?'

'You could both be right,' Laker said as he surveyed their surroundings. 'Them Injuns might be miles away like Sol reckons but I'd not hanker to bet my scalp on it.'

'They sure must be mad about me killing that young buck,' Brooks snorted. 'Who'd have figured that killing one stinking Injun could rile a whole tribe?'

'I had me a notion it might.' Laker sighed as he licked his dry lips.

'I'm for getting out of here.' Cohen swung his mount full circle and then stared at his fellow bank robbers. 'We'd best ride for Durango. I got me a gut feeling that it ain't no echo we're listening to, boys. Ben's right. They're close. Darn close.'

'Listen to them drums,' Brooks said as he waved his gun at every shadow. 'Them damn Injuns are plumb everywhere. All around us, just waiting to pick us off.'

Cohen steadied his horse. 'Let's go.

Hanging around here is darn suicidal. I ain't got me much hair but I'd like to keep what I got on my head.'

'We'll go when I say, Sol.' Brooks pulled back on his reins as his hooded eyes searched the area. 'I don't run scared from no snivelling Injuns. If they wanna fight, I'll oblige the bastards.'

'I don't reckon our chances too high if we stay here,' Laker told the outlaw leader.

'Jody's right, Ben,' Cohen agreed with the young outlaw. 'They might be closing in on us.'

Brooks nodded. 'OK. We ride but we don't run. I've never run from no critter with feathers in his hair and I ain't starting now.'

The heavily notched six-shooter hung from Brooks's hand as he readied himself for action. He turned the head of his horse and tapped his spurs. Cohen and Laker trailed their leader along the trail road toward the distant railhead.

'How many of them Kiowa do you

reckon are in this damn forest, Ben?' Cohen asked as he pulled out his tobacco pouch and started making a cigarette.

'Too many by the sound of it,' Laker put in first.

Brooks gritted his teeth.

'Just hush up and keep riding, boys,' he growled.

'Do you figure they got guns, Ben?' Cohen asked.

Brooks glanced at Cohen as their horses trotted down the moonlit trail. 'You'd be safer with a gun in your hand than them makings, Sol.'

Cohen looked around them as his tongue traced along the gummed edge of the cigarette paper.

'I reckon all they got is bows and arrows,' he said before placing the crude cigarette between his lips. 'They'd have to be pretty loco if they attacked us when we're so well armed.'

'You're right, Sol,' Brooks agreed and then laughed. 'I bet none of them critters got firepower like us. I reckon all they got is drums and piddling bows and arrows.'

Both Cohen and Laker roared with laughter.

The three horsemen tapped their spurs and increased their speed. Then suddenly the ominous sound of the pounding drums stopped.

The forest fell silent all around them as they made their way along the trail. The outlaws looked at one another in stunned surprise.

'How come the drums stopped, Ben?' Laker asked Brooks nervously. 'Why'd they stop drumming?'

Cohen pulled the crude cigarette from his mouth, crushed it in the palm of his hand and then tossed it aside. He grabbed his .45 and drew it.

'This ain't good, is it?' he mumbled.

Laker nodded as his eyes darted at the black trees which verged around the trail road. 'You're right, Sol. This ain't good at all.'

Curiously, Ben Brooks stood in his stirrups and went to speak when suddenly a more disturbing noise cut through the cold night air. It sounded like a thousand crazed hornets being released from their hive.

The eerie noise grew louder.

The merciless outlaw sat back down on his saddle as his fevered mind realized what they were hearing in the moonlit forest.

It was the chilling sound of arrows leaving bows and flying at speed through the air.

Brooks and Cohen fired their guns and whipped the tails of their horses feverishly in a bid to escape the avenging Kiowas' arrows. Laker bent over the neck of his mount and encouraged his horse to gallop.

Arrows rained in on the three horsemen from every angle as the Brooks gang attempted the impossible and outrun the lethal projectiles. No sooner had the outlaws' mounts responded to the frantic spurs of their masters when the arrows swooped in on their targets.

The brutal impact of the lethal projectiles hit the horsemen from every side. Cohen had an arrow buried deep in his thigh but he continued to fire his six-shooter into the trees before his gun hammer fell on spent casings. Only then did the wounded Cohen turn his mount and gallop away in the direction of the railhead.

Miraculously unscathed, Brooks continued to fire in all directions as he felt his mount collapsing beneath him. The outlaw leader hit the ground hard and somersaulted across the moonlit ground. He scrambled to his feet, pulled his other six-shooter from its holster and continued firing blindly as he made his way toward his stricken horse.

The moonlit sand was coloured dark crimson as blood poured from the animal's horrendous wounds but that meant nothing to the lethal Brooks. All he could think about was the canvas bank bag full of money tied to his saddle horn.

More arrows hurtled from the surrounding trees at their elusive target. Brooks ducked and crawled as the arrows embedded into the body of the horse and saddle. He fired again and then heard the sound of pounding hoofs. His hooded eyes glanced to his left and saw Laker riding back toward him. His bloody hand pulled his rifle free of the saddle scabbard and cocked its mechanism. Before Laker had brought his horse to a stop, Brooks grabbed the money bag from the saddle horn and tossed it over his shoulder.

Laker defied his own fear and rode up to Brooks. The young outlaw pulled his right boot out of the stirrup and held out his hand.

'Get up behind me, Ben,' he implored. 'Sol managed to escape but I reckon he's hurt bad.'

Brooks gripped Laker's forearm and was about to raise his boot and step into the stirrup when another flurry of feathered arrows cut through the gloom and gun smoke around them.

A sickening noise filled the moonlit trail as the youngest of the Brooks gang shook on his saddle.

'Aaaagh,' Laker screamed out and arched in agony as he was skewered by two of the Kiowas' arrows. Ruthlessly, Brooks looked up at the wounded outlaw and then tightened his grip on Laker's shaking arm.

'I'm hit, Ben,' Laker said as blood poured freely from his mouth. 'Help me.'

'I need your damn horse more than you do, Jody,' Brooks snarled before callously hauling the wounded Laker off his saddle.

The outlaw crashed into the ground at his cohort's boots. Blood sparkled in the moonlight as Brooks instantly replaced the youngster atop the nervous horse. Without a second thought he cocked his rifle, aimed it at the young outlaw and fired. Laker's head exploded.

'You should have kept riding, Jody. That's what I'd have done.'

Brooks gathered up the reins quickly, turned the horse and fired the rifle in his outstretched hand at their unseen enemies. The mount thundered away from the blood-stained ground with Brooks crouched across the three hefty money bags, still firing his Winchester back at his foes.

As arrows flew through the moonlight in pursuit of the fleeing rider, Brooks had only one thought on his mind. He had to reach the Durango railhead and ride the rails away from this bloodbath.

11

An eerie mist rose up from the frost-covered ground like a thousand spirits in search of sanctuary yet the rider of the powerful palomino did not notice any of them. All the gruesome bounty hunter could see was the tracks of those he hunted cut into the moonlit trail before him.

Iron Eyes had made good time from Ten Strike into the dense wooded hills south of the remote settlement. His prized mount had responded well to the few hours' rest its determined master had allowed it. Now, as it thundered through the moonlight and followed the tracks of the Brooks gang's horses, the high-shouldered palomino seemed to be gathering pace when lesser animals would have floundered.

The bounty hunter had not once needed to use his blood-stained spurs to encourage his mount. The powerful horse raced along the southern trail toward the distant railhead without any encouragement from its master.

The haunting figure navigated through the dense forest in pursuit of the three bank robbers with just one plan carved into his unholy mind.

To kill them and claim the bounty on their heads.

To Iron Eyes there was no other way. The posters said 'dead or alive' and to him that simply meant 'dead'. For he did not take prisoners.

The swift-footed stallion obeyed every unsaid command of the daunting man balanced in the stirrups above its muscular shoulders. All Iron Eyes had to do was move a muscle and the pure-bred stallion instantly understood what was expected of it.

Unlike the outlaws he chased, Iron Eyes had already learned that the next train out of Durango was not until the early hours of the morning. There was plenty of time to not only catch up with his prey, but to also kill them.

As Iron Eyes stood in his stirrups and leaned over the cream-coloured mane of his galloping mount, the scent of recently fired gun smoke filled his flared nostrils.

Like a ravenous wolf, he sensed his valiant mount was closing the distance on death itself.

Iron Eyes eased back on his reins and slowed his horse to a walk. Every honed instinct in his thin, emaciated body was warning him to be wary. He sniffed at the cold night air like a bloodhound and then lowered himself back down onto his highly decorated saddle. The tall palomino stallion walked steadily along the trail road as its silent master chewed on the smouldering cigar between his teeth.

His pupils darted around the strange scenery before him. Sam Parker had told him that the road led to only one place and that was the railhead at Durango but something was gnawing at his innards with every step of his golden horse's long legs.

Even hardened bounty hunters could fall into a well set trap, Iron Eyes thought. His eyes searched for any hint of a bushwhacker's gun in the shadows which encircled him.

The scent of death hung on the cold air. There was no mistaking the smell of gun smoke to a man that had lived his life either shooting or being shot at. As the muscular stallion continued to walk steadily along the winding trail, he knew that death was somewhere ahead.

He pulled the cigar from his lips and tossed it down at the dusty road. Smoke drifted through his small sharp teeth as the horse continued to walk ever closer to whatever had happened ahead of him.

Iron Eyes leaned against his ornate saddle cantle and studied the tall trees which flanked the trail road. He pulled a whiskey bottle from his saddlebags and eased its cork from the neck. He took a swig of the fiery contents and then saw something ahead of him which made him pull his long leathers up to his chest.

The crumpled moonlit shape was partly covered in frost.

The palomino stopped and stood like a statue as its master returned the cork to the bottle neck and patted it down. His eyes remained glued to the strange shape ahead of him as his bony fingers dropped the bottle back into the satchel.

With well-rehearsed expertise, Iron Eyes swung a long leg over the head of his horse and silently slid to the ground. He kept a firm grip on the reins and then slowly advanced forward.

The eerie light that only a large moon could cast down upon everything trapped below its strange illumination was dancing upon something ahead. Iron Eyes kept on striding toward the mysterious object.

Then it became obvious what had caught his attention.

The body of the young Kiowa brave

lay where Ben Brooks had left it. The crumpled Kiowa lay in the middle of a pool of congealing gore. The bounty hunter glanced around the trail road and recognized the familiar horse shoe marks left by the gang.

Iron Eyes knelt and ran a hand over the dead brave's face.

The shot had been deadly accurate, he thought. Iron Eyes rose back to his full height and then saw the pinto pony through the trees a few yards away from its downed master.

The gaunt figure pulled his reins toward him until the palomino stallion was at his shoulder. Iron Eyes was about to turn when his keen eyesight spotted something else marked on the sand. He lowered his head until his long black hair hung over his scarred features.

His eyes burned down onto the sand at the marks of moccasin tracks. A lot of moccasin tracks. It was clear that the Kiowa had discovered the body and set out after the men that had killed the young buck. Iron Eyes straightened up and ran his bony fingers through his hair as his eyes darted around the surrounding trees.

'Just like them smoke signals said. We ain't alone, horse,' the tall hunter of men whispered as he raised his long thin left leg and hoisted himself back up onto the saddle. 'Reckon we'd best be careful from here on. The last thing I wanna do is tangle with a herd of ornery Kiowa.'

Iron Eyes tapped his spurs and got the horse moving again.

As the stallion started to trot along the shadowy trail, the bounty hunter kept looking and listening for anything that did not seem normal.

Few places troubled the man that was said to be a living ghost but this terrain was different. This land troubled him because nothing was as he thought it should be. For one thing, he could not understand why there were Kiowa this far away from their ancestral homeland. The only reason that made any sense to Iron Eyes was that the entire tribe had been forcibly removed from their own land and planted here instead.

Why? Iron Eyes lashed his reins harder across the tail of the trotting horse as he rode deeper into the land he neither understood nor trusted.

He had ridden a few miles when he caught the scent of recently fired guns again. Iron Eyes stopped his palomino again and searched the trees and bushes for any sign of the warriors he felt sure were close.

If they were nearby, Iron Eyes could not sense or see them. He turned his tall horse and moved closer to the trees as he trailed the growing scent of gun smoke.

The tall horse walked slowly but its thin rider knew that the thoroughbred was like a coiled spring and ready to burst into action whenever he spurred. Using the shadows along the road for cover, Iron Eyes continued to quietly urge the stallion forward.

For another mile the horse obeyed its master and kept on to where the smell of the recently fired guns still lingered on the night air. Then as the palomino rounded a corner, Iron Eyes saw the very thing he had been looking for.

His bullet coloured eyes focused on the macabre sight.

The blood seemed to cover half of the trail road. Lying in the heart of the moonlit gore he spied another body but this one was totally different to the previous one he had found. This was a white man.

Iron Eyes drew back on his reins and stopped the horse's progress as he studied the lifeless horse twenty feet away from the dead man.

The acrid smell of death might have been fresh but it still unnerved the palomino beneath him. It took every ounce of his horsemanship just to control the powerful animal. Iron Eyes drew the reins up to his chest as he dropped one of his hands into his trail coat pocket and pulled the Navy Colt free of the loose bullets.

He cocked its hammer and then dismounted the skittish stallion. Iron Eyes tied his reins to a tree branch and looked around the area. Then the gaunt bounty hunter took three paces toward the pool of blood and looked down at the horrific scene.

Just like the dead carcass of the horse, the body was filled with arrows. Iron Eyes surveyed the moonlit area around the Jody Laker's remains. There were arrows everywhere.

Iron Eyes walked across the bloody ground to where the corpse lay and stared down at it. He focused hard on the body. Although filled with several arrows it was the unrecognizable head of the body which drew the bounty hunter's attention the most.

This was not the work of any kind of Indian that he knew of. No Indian of any tribe would fire a shot into the face of its already doomed prey, he told himself. Whoever had blown the outlaw's face to bits was no Kiowa.

Iron Eyes sighed heavily and gritted his teeth.

Every sinew in his lean frame knew that this was Ben Brooks's handiwork. Iron Eyes had heard too many stories about the bank robber to doubt his merciless traits. Brooks had killed both the men in the bank even though they were unarmed and basically helpless.

Iron Eyes imagined that it was Brooks who had also used his venomous accuracy to destroy the young Kiowa brave. The bounty hunter shook his head angrily. It was not the mindless killing that angered Iron Eyes the most. It was the fact that Brooks had made it impossible to prove that this was one of the wanted outlaws.

Iron Eyes had been cheated by one of the men he was hunting and that riled him. Brooks had robbed him of a valuable bounty.

Like a monstrous nightmare in human form, Iron Eyes turned and strode back across the bloody ground back to his powerful mount. The blood had grown sticky on the moonlit ground and stuck to his boot leather.

Iron Eyes rubbed his boots on the dry sand beside his horse when his keen hearing heard something beyond the wall of trees and bushes.

His bony hand lifted the Navy Colt and rested it against his shoulder as his eyes searched for whatever had caught his attention. He then backed up against the palomino and lifted his free hand until his bony fingers found and grabbed hold of the silver saddle horn.

'Reckon we got company, horse,' he whispered as he mounted the stallion in one fluid action. Iron Eyes kept the gun aimed at the place where he had heard the sound as his right hand pulled his long leathers free of the tree branch.

The bounty hunter steadied the powerful horse and wrapped the reins around his wrist as his unblinking eyes continued to burn across the trail.

Suddenly he saw them. At least three feathered Kiowa braves emerged from the cover of the trees and unleashed their arrows at the unholy apparition.

'Hell!' Iron Eyes cursed as three lethal projectiles cut through the moonlight toward him. Although the arrows were travelling at speed, the horseman's stallion bolted into action even faster.

Iron Eyes hung onto the saddle horn and blasted his Navy Colt in response. The intrepid horse thundered away from shadows in a bid to escape the deadly attack. The stallion was galloping before any of the Kiowa arrows were embedded into the tree trunks.

As more arrows flew after the fleeing palomino, the bounty hunter hung low over the neck of his horse and emptied the gun at his attackers. Hidden by the fresh gun smoke and rising mist, the powerful stallion somehow managed to escape the Kiowa war bows' fury.

Iron Eyes did not slow his pace for more than two miles and only straightened up on his saddle when he felt the stallion start to flag after such a valiant bid to outrun its master's enemies. He pulled back on his reins and then turned on his saddle and stared back at the hoof dust behind them.

The stallion slowed back to a walk as Iron Eyes looked around them and hastily reloaded the still smoking six-shooter. His eyes then stared back at the ground.

A cruel smile etched his hideous features as he saw the two sets of fresh hoof tracks on the sand. Iron Eyes recognized them both as belonging to the outlaws' mounts.

A hundred miles had branded them into his mind.

Then as the stallion approached another bend in the trail road, something alerted the palomino beneath him. The stallion shied and stopped as another saddle horse came galloping wildly around the corner. The wide-eyed horse collided into the bounty hunter's stallion.

The ghost-like horseman grabbed at the animal's loose leathers and dragged it to a sudden halt beside his tall palomino. Iron Eyes looked down at the blood-covered saddle and then released his grip.

This was another of the outlaw's horses, he thought.

And by the state of the saddle, its rider had not been as lucky as the gaunt bounty hunter. Iron Eyes released his grip on the horse, wiped the blood from the palms of his hands down the front to his long coat and then spurred and grimly rode forward.

The powerful stallion trotted around the corner as its master kept a firm grip on the Navy Colt. The horse continued on into the shadowy depths of the trail as the bounty hunter stared ahead in search of the last two outlaws and the bank money they had escaped Ten Strike with.

For what felt like an eternity, Iron Eyes did not see or hear a thing. Then as the palomino reached a clearing at the foot of a hill, the bounty hunter saw what was left of Sol Cohen stretched out on a grassy verge.

'Not another damn body.'

Iron Eyes rode toward the lifeless Cohen. The outlaw was in a heap beneath the telling moon. As the notorious horseman neared the body, he saw the face of the dead outlaw looking up at the cloudless night sky with glazed eyes.

He slid the six-shooter behind his belt buckle and wrapped his reins around the silver saddle horn.

The bounty hunter dismounted and moved to above Cohen. He had never seen a face so drained of colour before. Then Iron Eyes looked to where the arrow had gone through the outlaw's thigh. Cohen's pants leg was soaking wet with the blood he had lost after being hit by the Kiowa arrow.

Every drop of Cohen's life's blood had poured from the savage wound in his leg. He was satisfied that at least this outlaw was still recognizable.

'I'll collect the bounty on you later,' he whispered.

Iron Eyes shook his head and then

turned back to where his horse waited. He strode back to the high shouldered animal and rested a bony hand on the silver saddle horn. He slid his boot into his stirrup and mounted. He glanced down at the body bathed in moonlight.

'You'll keep until I ride back this way, amigo,' he told the corpse coldly. 'Reckon by the looks of it, Ben Brooks has gotten all the money again. Now ain't that a surprise?'

His eyes focused to the top of the rise. The night sky seemed to be glowing just above the horizon. He stood in his stirrups and squinted hard at the glowing light before satisfying himself at what he was looking at.

'That's gotta be the Durango rail-head lights,' he muttered as his bony hand held his mount in check. 'C'mon, horse. We gotta kill us a varmint and collect some money.'

Iron Eyes pulled one of his Navy Colts from behind his belt buckle and cocked its hammer. His eyes screwed up as they focused on the glowing lights.

He cracked the long leathers at the ground and got his magnificent stallion moving. Within a few heartbeats, the palomino had reached a gallop.

Although Iron Eyes did not have any idea how far it was to the railhead, he knew that was where he would find the outlaw he had tracked for the last hundred miles.

Like a moth drawn to a naked flame, Iron Eyes kept on riding toward the tell-tale sign of the distant lights as they lit up the hill top.

Apart from the sound of the horse being carefully steered through the dense scenery, there were no other noises. Not one living creature dared to make a sound in case the man who carried death on his shoulders turned his weaponry on them instead.

The palomino stallion gathered pace.

Iron Eyes kept the cocked six-shooter aimed at the glowing lights as his horse continued to close the distance between the railhead and himself.

As the powerful stallion continued heading toward the railhead lights, Iron Eyes placed a cigar between his lips and scratched a match with his thumbnail and cupped its flame to its tip. Smoke trailed over the wide shoulders of the gaunt rider as he neared the crest of the hill.

Iron Eyes raised a skinny hand, pulled the cigar from his scarred lips and exhaled a line of grey smoke. His eyes narrowed as the stallion reached the top of the hill.

The bounty hunter steadied the palomino and looked down at the railhead set on the outskirts of the sprawling Durango with a cruel glint in his unblinking eyes. Every one of his senses knew that somewhere down there, among the metal tracks and buildings, was the last of the gang he sought.

Iron Eyes could almost smell Ben Brooks.

'He's down there, horse,' the bounty hunter whispered as he noticed the lantern lit railhead. 'All we gotta do is find and kill the bastard.'

He reached back and pulled a whiskey bottle from his saddlebags. His teeth gripped its cork and dragged it free.

Iron Eyes spat the cork at the ground and drained the bottle's contents. As the strong fumes filled his flared nostrils, he threw the glass vessel over his shoulder and then held his cigar between his teeth. He inhaled deeply and then spat it at the dust.

'Let's do this, horse,' he growled. 'Let's get him.'

12

Iron Eyes slapped the animal into motion with the tails of his reins. His emaciated body hung on to his long leathers as the palomino stallion thundered down toward the railhead bathed in the amber light of its numerous lanterns. Few men had ever seen the infamous bounty hunter charging toward them with a fully loaded six-gun in his hand.

Even fewer had lived to tell the tale.

The eerie moonlight only increased the horror which thundered down across the steep slope like a living corpse fleeing the fiery inferno his undead spirit had just escaped from. No monstrous nightmare could have appeared quite so daunting as the sight of his scarred face that stared with unblinking eyes at the array of wooden structures set around the gleaming rail tracks.

This was no ordinary man who sat astride the thundering stallion with one of his famed Navy Colts in his skeletal hand. This was something far more deadly that rode like a bat out of Hell after his latest prey.

As the powerful horse galloped beneath him, Iron Eyes stared at the scattering of wooden structures in search of Ben Brooks.

The famed hunter of men navigated the magnificent palomino through the tall grass and between the trees and yet did not seem to move a muscle.

Iron Eyes thrust his blood-stained spurs into the flanks of the high-shouldered stallion as the scent of his prey filled his flared nostrils. The galloping horse ate up the ground between itself and the railhead at unimaginable speed, while its master watched the quiet railhead for any sign of Ben Brooks and the money he had stolen from the bank at Ten Strike.

Then, as the golden stallion neared

the railhead, a shot rang out from the shadows of the largest of the wooden buildings.

Iron Eyes had seen the red hot taper of lethal lead cut a course toward him a heartbeat before he heard the deafening sound of the rifle shot.

The bullet hurtled toward the approaching rider and caught Iron Eyes in his right shoulder. He was knocked sideways by the impact of the bullet and nearly fell from his high perch as he saw another red hot taper cutting through the moonlight toward him. Iron Eyes ducked as the bullet passed inches over his head.

He was now less than fifty yards from the shadowy main building but knew he was a sitting duck on top of his muscular stallion.

Iron Eyes leapt from his saddle. His boots hit the ground and he rolled over a few times before coming to a rest close to a tree amid tall dry grass. Venomously, Iron Eyes fired a shot into the shadows and then watched his stallion trot to safety.

'That horse must be smarter than me,' the bounty hunter hissed as he fired another shot into the depths of the shadows. 'He knows when to quit.'

Brooks fired two more rifle shots in quick succession from his hiding place at the very end of the long structure. The bullets came so close to hitting the bounty hunter, Iron Eyes felt their heat as they skimmed over his scalp.

'I gotta get closer,' Iron Eyes said as he got to his knees. 'I ain't got the range that his Winchester has.'

Iron Eyes raised the Navy Colt and squeezed its trigger in reply and then threw himself down the slope. He rolled over and rested his back against a well-nourished tree. Brooks let loose with another volley of lethal lead.

A deafening crescendo of rifle shots filled the night air as chunks of the tree bark were torn from its trunk. Iron Eyes was showered in smouldering sawdust as his sharp eyes stared across at the rifle smoke drifting from the side of the long building.

He knew that Brooks was still beyond the range of his Navy Colt. He had to get closer if he were to be able to hit his target.

Iron Eyes slowly stood behind the tree.

Brooks fired another handful of shots at the gaunt bounty hunter. Again Iron Eyes heard the sound of the deadly accurate bullets tear bark from the tree trunk's surface.

'Another shot or two and that rifle will need reloading,' the emaciated man hunter murmured as he looked at his shoulder and saw the hole in his coat. He pushed the smoking barrel of his gun under the weathered material and lifted it.

His eyes stared at the graze. Although it was bleeding freely, Iron Eyes realized how lucky he had come. He flexed his fingers and pulled his other Navy Colt from his deep bullet-filled pocket.

He cocked both guns and waited.

Two more rifle shots came from

Brooks's Winchester and splintered off the side of the tree. Iron Eyes's keen hearing heard the tell-tale sound of the rifle's hammer falling on the empty rifle magazine.

That was what he had been waiting for.

Faster than a hound chasing a fox, Iron Eyes dashed across the clearing toward the long building. He knew that it takes time to reload a repeating rifle. A lot more time than it takes to reload a six-shooter.

The panting bounty hunter pressed his back against the wall at the opposite end of the long structure. He leaned around and fired two shots down to the opposite end of the building.

Brooks fired back, taking the corner off the side wall beside Iron Eyes's head. A knowing smile came to the mutilated features of the bounty hunter.

Iron Eyes fired again into the distant shadows and heard his bullet ricochet off something. He did not attempt looking to see what it was he had hit because he knew it was not the outlaw.

Another few rifle shots blasted at the structure he was resting beside. The smell of burning wood shavings filled the air beside the emaciated figure. Another chunk of the wall had been whittled off the corner of the building.

Iron Eyes responded by firing his Colts four times at the outlaw and then swung back and shook the spent casings from both his guns. As his long thin fingers plucked fresh bullets from his deep trail coat pocket and filled his smoking chambers, he saw another few shots rip even more wood from the building's corner.

He snapped both his guns shut and pushed their ramrods back into position and then cocked their hammers.

Over and over Iron Eyes fired and cocked his guns until the air was full of choking smoke.

'How'd you know I was after you, Brooks?' Iron Eyes yelled out from his hiding place. 'Or don't it matter none to you if you kill innocent drifters?'

'I heard the shooting back there,' Brooks shouted back. 'I figured you had to be on my trail to be riding through Injun country. Reckon you must be all that's left of a posse, huh?'

'Nope,' Iron Eyes disagreed loudly. 'I ain't no posse.'

Ben Brooks paused for a moment and frowned. 'How'd you know my name?'

'I know the name of every varmint I hunt, Brooks,' Iron Eyes shouted at the top of his lungs. 'I also know how much you're worth dead or alive.'

A cold shiver traced the outlaw's spine.

'Are you a stinking bounty hunter?' Brooks snarled. 'Is that what you are? A stinking bounty hunter?'

'Yep, there ain't nobody stinks as good as me,' Iron Eyes's voice echoed around the buildings. 'I reckon you'll get a good whiff just before I kill you.'

Troubled by the seemingly fearless man that he had so far failed to kill, Brooks edged away from the wooden building back to where he had secured his mount and pulled the three canvas bags off its shoulders. His eyes glanced up at a large, white-faced clock dial and wondered when the next train would arrive for him to make his escape with his loot.

'You ready to die yet?' the haunting voice of Iron Eyes rang out in the night air. 'If you are, I'll oblige.'

'You're the one that's gonna die.' Brooks raised his rifle and fired another shot down at the corner of the long building. There was no reply. Not a single shot came from the bounty hunter. Brooks fired his rifle again and again but his tormentor did not respond.

The outlaw was troubled.

Brooks carried the swollen money bags across the gleaming rails to the other side of the tracks.

As the outlaw rested his back against a red brick wall and pushed bullets from his gun belt into the magazine of the Winchester, he heard the sound of spurs echoing all around him. His hooded eyes darted as he cocked his rifle.

'Are you ready to die yet, Brooks?' Iron Eyes yelled out again.

The haunting voice gnawed into the outlaw's mind. Brooks pressed his back up against the wall and frowned.

'I'm gonna kill you slow, stranger,' Brooks screamed in reply. 'Slow and painful.'

Suddenly there was no sound at all. No mocking voice or jangling spurs for the deadly outlaw to aim his rifle barrel toward.

Brooks swallowed hard as his mind raced. 'Who are you?'

Suddenly the voice of the bounty hunter travelled across the void between them.

'They call me Iron Eyes!'

The infamous name chilled the outlaw to the bone. He, like most of the wanted men in the West, knew of the name and feared it. To be hunted by Iron Eyes was as good as having a noose around your neck. Outlaws stood more chance with the Grim Reaper on their trail than Iron Eyes.

Sweat trailed down Brooks's face as his hooded eyes looked at the railroad tracks and wondered when the train would arrive. He knew that he could not hide from the deadly bounty hunter all night.

'What you after me for, Iron Eyes?' Brooks shouted out.

'For the bounty on your head,' Iron Eyes retorted.

Brooks turned and looked along the wall to where he suspected the voice was coming from. He placed the money bags at his boots and lifted the rifle and held it up against his shoulder.

'How'd it be with you if I let you have some of this loot, Iron Eyes?' Brooks shouted out as he waited for a glimpse of the bounty hunter. 'I got more money here than I'm worth on any of them wanted posters.'

There was a long silence. Brooks moved away from the wall and clutched the money bags tightly as he crouched behind a buckboard.

'Reckon you're tempted, Iron Eyes,' Brooks called out again. 'I bet you're thinking about it, huh?'

Again there was no reply. The outlaw cocked the hand guard of his rifle again and strained to see his adversary in the shadows. There was no sign of the gaunt bounty hunter.

'Why don't you answer?' Brooks called out through the frosty mist in frustration as his index finger stroked the rifle trigger of his primed weapon.

Suddenly, without warning, Iron Eyes appeared on the roof above the outlaw. Brooks swung around and saw the ominous figure upon the flat roof of the weathered structure. The deadly outlaw fired his rifle at the haunting vision as terror raced through Brooks's veins.

Iron Eyes did not move a muscle as the ragged tails of his long dust coat were lifted by the bullet. Then like some mystical creature, he jumped down on Brooks before the bank robber could fire his Winchester a second time.

The mule-eared boots knocked Brooks off his feet. Both men flew off the crude platform and crashed on the moonlit rail tracks. They scrambled like savage wolves on the tracks, exchanging blows until Brooks landed a brutal uppercut which connected with Iron Eyes's jaw.

The dazed bounty hunter fell backwards as the taste of blood filled his mouth. He narrowed his eyes and watched his opponent stagger to his rifle and snatch it from beside the metal tracks.

Iron Eyes leapt to his side as Brooks fired.

The entire yard lit up as a blinding flame spewed from the Winchester barrel. Iron Eyes felt the heat of the bullet as it passed close to his face.

Without a moment's hesitation, the emaciated bounty hunter threw himself through the choking gun smoke and caught Brooks around the middle.

Both men fell heavily on to the

tracks. Iron Eyes pounded the face of his foe mercilessly until his knuckles were bleeding. Then Brooks brought the metal barrel of his rifle up and lashed its length across the bounty hunter's skull.

The sound of the crushing blow resonated around the wooden buildings to both sides of the brawling men. Iron Eyes slumped as Brooks pushed his painfully thin body off him.

With blood pouring from the gashes across his face, Brooks got back to his feet and primed his rifle. Before the bank robber had time to squeeze its trigger, Iron Eyes had used his long legs to sweep Brooks off his feet again.

As the still groggy Brooks landed, the Winchester blasted another venomous bullet up into the moonlit heavens. Iron Eyes staggered to his feet and pulled his matched pair of Navy Colts free of his belt and deep coat pocket.

The exhausted bounty hunter stared through his mane of limp black hair at the man on the ground before him. He fired one of his guns and tore the rifle from Brooks's grip.

His bloody foe glared up at the hideous sight above him as the rifle clattered across the rail tracks. His hooded eyes glared at Iron Eyes as he thought about the .45s he still had holstered around his girth.

'I reckon this is it, Brooks. I'm through playing games with your sorrowful hide.'

Brooks steadied himself and flexed his fingers over his holstered six-shooters.

'You can't shoot me in cold blood, Iron Eyes,' he growled at the bounty hunter. 'Not even a stinking hombre like you would kill an unarmed man.'

Iron Eyes grinned dangerously.

'You ain't unarmed, Brooks,' he hissed like a rattler. 'You got the same amount of guns as me. The only difference is that mine are in my hands.'

Brooks was confused. 'What's that meant to mean?'

'It means you're dead.' Iron Eyes

squeezed on both his triggers and sent two bullets roaring into the bank robber.

The deafening shots lit up the railhead for a fraction of a second. It was long enough for the bounty hunter to see both his bullets hit the wanted outlaw dead centre.

As the crumpled body of Ben Brooks fell at his feet, Iron Eyes whistled and then stared down at the lifeless outlaw.

'I showed you the same mercy that you showed them pitiful critters back along the trail.' Iron Eyes sneered and spat blood at his prize. 'Sometimes you gotta sink your fangs into a sidewinder before he bites you.'

The palomino stallion trotted up to its master and snorted at the ground. Iron Eyes picked up the three money bags and hung them from his silver saddle horn.

Iron Eyes then grabbed Brooks's collar and dragged him out to where he had left his saddle horse.

The gaunt bounty hunter was covered in his opponent's gore by the time he had draped Brooks over the saddle and tied his hands and boots together.

Iron Eyes mounted the tall palomino and then reached across to the saddle horse. His bony hand took hold of Brooks's horse's long leathers.

He then opened a fresh bottle of whiskey and poured some of the hard liquor into the palm of his hand and rubbed it over his grazed shoulder. He downed a long swallow and rested the bottle on his thigh.

'Now all we gotta do is go pick up his pal and ride back to Ten Strike, horse,' Iron Eyes said as the powerful stallion started to retrace the route it had taken to reach the railhead. 'Sure hope them Kiowa don't kick up a fuss, though. There ain't no profit in killing Injuns.'

As Iron Eyes led the saddle horse away from the railroad tracks, he heard the sound of a train whistle echo in the night air. He looked at the body draped over the saddle behind his golden mount and grinned.

'The train's early, Brooks,' he told the corpse. 'Looks like you're gonna miss it, though.'

Finale

The people of Ten Strike were as joyful as any Iron Eyes had ever seen when he delivered the three money bags to them and dragged the bodies of Ben Brooks and Sol Cohen to the newly appointed sheriff's office. They had paid him the sum he had agreed and also given him a chit for the delivery of the dead outlaws.

With a long cigar between his teeth, Iron Eyes filled his pants pocket with the rolled wad of bills and the chit he would redeem for hard cash when he reached a town authorized to pay him the reward money. The tall figure had not spoken more than a few words since he had arrived back in Ten Strike with his valuable cargo.

All he could do was wonder how he had managed to avoid the Kiowas' deadly arrows unscathed. He took the long reins of his handsome golden stallion and headed for the only place in the sun-baked town to offer some respite from the blazing sun.

The morning sun burned into his wounded body as he walked to the river and sat down on its muddy bank. He was dog-tired and it showed. He had rented a room in the hotel again and this time intended to stay there until his wounds had healed.

The palomino lowered its head and started to drink from the crystal clear river as Iron Eyes enjoyed his cigar.

'I'll give the blacksmith an extra few bucks to take good care of you, horse.' Iron Eyes sighed wearily, pulling the cigar from his lips. 'If you weren't so damn fast I'd have lost my scalp back there.'

Suddenly the stallion stopped drinking. It raised its head and stared along the river as droplets of water dripped from its white chin.

'What's wrong, horse?' the bounty hunter asked the palomino and then cast his attention to where the stallion's eyes were focused. Iron Eyes raised a hand and shielded his eyes from the bright glare that danced across the water.

The sight that met his eyes surprised and chilled him to the bone. Iron Eyes tossed the cigar aside and then allowed his coat to fall from his bony shoulders. The bounty hunter waded out into the river toward the strange object which was floating toward him.

The closer it got the more his heart pounded.

Iron Eyes stood waist deep in the cool water and waited for the large chunk of wood to float toward him. For the first time in a long while he was frightened. Yet it was not the chunk of wood which troubled him. It was the sight of the tiny female lying face down upon it that tore at his very fibre.

As the wood came to a halt beside him, he immediately realized what it was. It was the roof of Squirrel Sally's stagecoach. His face drained of colour as his long thin arms stretched out until his fingers could grab her. He slid her near naked body across the wet surface toward him and then turned her over.

His thin fingers frantically combed her wet hair off her face and stared in disbelief at her. She was cut all over but the river had washed the blood away.

His heart was beating so hard inside his chest that he imagined it would burst. Terror gripped him as he vainly patted her cheek.

'Don't you damn well die, Squirrel,' he hissed.

Iron Eyes scooped the petite form up in his arms and held her close to him. He waded back to the riverbank and staggered up to where the palomino stallion stood watching its master.

The bounty hunter fell on to one knee and lowered her down gently. His eyes glanced over her perfect body and then pressed his hand under her left breast in search of a heartbeat. All he could feel was her cold skin. He swallowed hard and looked all around them. For the first time in his sorrowful existence, he needed someone to tell him what to do but there was nobody even close to the riverbank.

Not wanting her skin to burn under the merciless sun, he dragged his blood-stained coat over her exposed body. His mutilated face stared down at her helplessly.

What had happened, his mind silently screamed.

Tears ran down his scarred cheeks as his fingers touched her face fearfully. She was colder than the dead outlaws he had just delivered.

Then to his utter surprise she opened her eyes and tore the coat off her. The startled Iron Eyes almost jumped out of his skin.

'You ain't dead,' he stammered.

'Of course I ain't dead, you long-legged fool,' Sally snapped before sitting up and staring at her naked upper half. 'And what have you done with my shirt? You thieved it, didn't you? Admit it. You was interfering with me. I take me a little shuteye and suddenly there you are playing with my chests again.'

Iron Eyes raised his eyebrows.

'You was floating out there,' he said.

'Did you touch my chests?' Sally asked firmly.

He shrugged. 'I . . . I guess so but I thought you was dead, Squirrel.'

'That's kinda sick, Iron Eyes.' She sighed. 'Taking advantage of a gal just cos you figure she won't object, being dead and all.'

Iron Eyes raised his hands. 'Honest, I found you like this. I ain't touched you or stole your shirt.'

'And why didn't you touch me?' Sally pulled him nearer and stared into his eyes. 'We is betrothed, you know. You got the right.'

Utterly confused, Iron Eyes felt her embrace him tightly and then start to sob into his scarred flesh. He raised a hand and started patting her back.

'What happened to you, Squirrel?' he whispered into her hair. 'Where are your horses and stagecoach? Don't tell me that lump of wood is all that's left.'

'We got hit off the trail by a waterfall.' Sally shivered at the memory. 'Damned if I know how I'm still alive.'

'You're too damn stubborn to die that easy,' Iron Eyes told her and touched her chin. 'Thank goodness.'

She pushed him back and frowned seductively. 'You owe me a new stagecoach, Iron Eyes. It's all your fault. If you hadn't have run off I'd not have had to trail you and got tangled up in that waterfall.'

He nodded. 'OK. I'll get you a new one and horses and whatever else you want. Just don't go scaring me like this again.'

'I surely love you.' Sally started to sob again as relief overwhelmed her battered and bruised form. Her arms embraced him and dragged his head into her cleavage. 'I figured I was gonna die, Iron Eyes.'

'And I thought you were dead when I seen you floating out there on that chunk of lumber, Squirrel.' He admitted. 'I ain't never felt that way before.'

'What way?' Sally asked.

'Alone,' he said. 'I felt plumb alone.'

Squirrel Sally was about to speak again when Iron Eyes took her by her shoulders and looked into her beautiful face for the longest while. He smiled as best he could. She closed her eyes and puckered her lips expectantly.

He kissed her forehead gently and then stood. 'Stay there till I get back.'

Disappointed, the female arched an eyebrow.

'Was that it?' she asked as he started to walk back into the middle of Ten Strike. 'Where the hell are you going, you ugly galoot?'

Iron Eyes looked over his shoulder. 'I'm going to buy you something you really want, Squirrel.'

'A diamond ring?' Sally grinned.

'Nope,' Iron Eyes replied. 'A brand new shirt.'

'A shirt.' Sally repeated and sat cross-legged beside his battered trail coat. She pulled a cigar from one of its deep pockets and placed it between her teeth. She chewed on its black length and shrugged. 'Get me a rifle as well. Then I can shoot you.'

We do hope that you have enjoyed reading this large print book.

Did you know that all of our titles are available for purchase?

We publish a wide range of high quality large print books including:
Romances, Mysteries, Classics
General Fiction
Non Fiction and Westerns

Special interest titles available in large print are:
The Little Oxford Dictionary
Music Book, Song Book
Hymn Book, Service Book

Also available from us courtesy of Oxford University Press:
Young Readers' Dictionary
(large print edition)
Young Readers' Thesaurus
(large print edition)

For further information or a free brochure, please contact us at:
Ulverscroft Large Print Books Ltd.,
The Green, Bradgate Road, Anstey,
Leicester, LE7 7FU, England.
Tel: (00 44) **0116 236 4325**
Fax: (00 44) **0116 234 0205**

HARPS FOR A WANTED GUN

Ty Walker

Cy Harper, a youngster in search of a job, rides across the infamous desert known as Satan's Lair toward the isolated town of Apache Pass. As he reaches the midway point of the perilous ocean of sand, rifle bullets start to rain down on him. Mistaking Harper for a hired gunman known as Lightning Luke Cooper, more than a dozen unknown riders chase his high-shouldered black stallion for hours and keep firing. Finally, one of their bullets catches him. Is this the end for the innocent drifter?